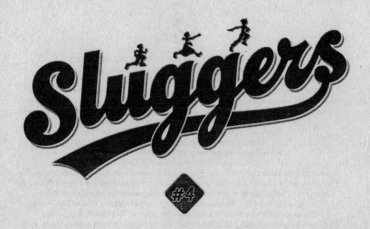

Sluggers

#4

WATER, WATER EVERYWHERE

LOREN LONG & PHIL BILDNER

SIMON & SCHUSTER BOOKS FOR YOUNG READERS
NEW YORK   LONDON   TORONTO   SYDNEY

SIMON & SCHUSTER BOOKS FOR YOUNG READERS
An imprint of Simon & Schuster Children's Publishing Division
1230 Avenue of the Americas, New York, New York 10020
This book is a work of fiction. Any references to historical events, real people, or real locales are used fictitiously. Other names, characters, places, and incidents are products of the author's imagination, and any resemblance to actual events or locales or persons, living or dead, is entirely coincidental.

Also available in a hardcover edition.
Book design by Jessica Handelman and Dan Potash • Hand lettering by Mark Simonson
The text for this book is set in Century 731 BT.
The illustrations for this book are rendered in charcoal.
Manufactured in the United States of America / 0413 OFF
First paperback edition January 2010
2 4 6 8 10 9 7 5 3
The Library of Congress has cataloged the hardcover edition as follows:
Library of Congress Cataloging-in-Publication Data
Long, Loren.
Water, water everywhere / Loren Long and Phil Bildner. — 1st ed.
p. cm. — (Sluggers ; 4)
"This is the fourth book in the Sluggers series
(previously published as Barnstormers)."
Summary: In 1899, in Minneapolis, Ruby Payne's decision to ask African American Preacher Wil to join the team causes division among the other players, and the magical baseball will not work unless the team is united.
ISBN 978-1-4169-1866-0 (hardcover)
[1. Baseball—Fiction. 2. Supernatural—Fiction. 3. Race relations—Fiction. 4. African Americans—Fiction. 5. Brothers and sisters—Fiction. 6. Minneapolis (Minn.)—History—19th century—Fiction.] I. Bildner, Phil. II. Title.
PZ7.L8555Wat 2009
[Fic]—dc22
2008016728
ISBN 978-1-4169-1890-5 (pbk) • ISBN 978-1-4391-5942-2 (eBook)

To Jim Bouton,
Curt Flood,
Kirby Puckett,
Marvin Miller,
Jackie Robinson,
and all the other
believers in baseball
and keepers of what is right.
—P. B.

To my father,
William G. Long,
who introduced me
to the Big Red Machine.
I'd still rather go to a ball game
with you than anyone.
—L. L.

Pregame Recap for

WATER, WATER EVERYWHERE

★

At their fiery performance in Chicago, the Travelin' Nine came out on top, burning through the competition and earning a much-needed victory. Using the baseball their uncle Owen had given them, Griffith, Ruby, and Graham Payne helped the team with magic that could only be found in the hot town of Chicago.

The barnstormers' first loss in Cincinnati, their stampede to victory in Louisville, combined with their blazing win in Chicago has prepared them for their next challenge in Minneapolis. Maybe this team will be able to earn enough money to pay off the Payne family debt after all. . . . But first they still must face huge hurdles in Illinois. Happy, the barnstormers' pitcher, collapsed at the end of the last inning and will not be able to play again. The team is now short a man and they can't afford to miss any games. What's more, Ruby vanished right before departure. Where could she be? Could the Chancellor have something to do with her disappearance?

Anxious about Ruby, Griffith is also reeling from his late-night encounter with the Chancellor. The man knows about the magic baseball and is plotting to get it. But what else does the Chancellor want from Griffith? And what could the Chancellor possibly have that Griffith wants?

★

Contents

"I call him Dog."

PROLOGUE

★

An Angel Looks for Answers

"Please be here," Ruby whis-pered to herself, approaching the gates of Jackson Park. She gripped the baseball in her side pocket as tightly as she ever had. She hadn't lifted a finger from it since leaving the train station.

By now, the others were surely frantic. She hadn't told her mother, either of her brothers, or any of the Travelin' Nine ballists that she was heading to the park. She hadn't told anyone that she was going anywhere. She just went.

BALLIST: *player.*

In her mind, Ruby could see their troubled expressions. She pictured her older brother, Griffith, grimacing as he tugged on his hair. She saw the worry lines around her mother's eyes deepen. And she saw the blank stares of Scribe, Woody, and all the other barnstormers as they tried to mask their concern.

Ruby hated sneaking off like this, but they would never have allowed her to go otherwise. This was her only chance. This was *their* only chance.

BARNSTORMERS: *team that tours an area playing exhibition games for moneymaking entertainment.*

She had left the downtown Chicago train station because she needed to find Preacher Wil. With Happy too ill to play, the barnstormers needed a new ballist. And Ruby believed with all her heart that Preacher Wil was that player.

Preacher Wil would be here. When they had first met at Jackson Park, he had told her he had a feeling their paths would cross in the future.

Maybe at this park again. Or perhaps even at your game.

Ruby had seen him at the game, but their paths had hardly crossed. He had waved to her from across the field and then mysteriously disappeared.

Entering the park, she headed straight for the plaque in front of the lagoon, the spot where they'd met. She would wait for him there. If he showed—*when* he showed—that's where he would be.

But Ruby didn't have to wait. He was already there. Even though his back was to her, Ruby recognized his form from across the plaza.

"Preacher Wil!" she shouted, racing over.

He turned. "Angel!" he exclaimed, wearing his warm smile. "Everything okay?"

"I knew you'd be here." She exhaled a breath of relief and, for the first time all morning, lifted her hand from the baseball.

"How'd you know?"

But before Ruby could answer, Preacher Wil's dog nestled up against her leg. She bent down, and the short-haired hound with the grayish coat and the black spots licked her neck and earlobe.

"What's his name?" Ruby giggled.

"He hasn't told me yet."

Ruby furrowed her brow. "So what do you call him?"

"I call him Dog," Preacher Wil replied, stroking his cheek with his thumb and the three remaining fingers of his left hand. "Angel, are you here by yourself?"

"Yes," she said, looking up.

"Do the others know you're here?"

She didn't answer.

"Angel"—he pinched the corners of his mouth and then pointed down at her—"do the others know you're here?"

"No." Ruby shook her head and stood back up.

"You must go back."

"You must come with . . ."

Preacher Wil tilted his head. "Come with . . . ?"

"Yes," said Ruby, gazing into his soft, comforting eyes. "That's why I'm here. You belong with us."

"I don't quite understand." Preacher Wil rested his rugged right hand on Dog's head. "How do you know?"

"I'm not sure," Ruby answered, slipping her hand back into her pocket. "I can't quite put my finger on it. I wanted to come looking for you at the game, but Griff wouldn't let me. Where did you go?"

"I was right," said Preacher Wil with a knowing smile. "You sure do like to ask questions."

"And you sure don't like to answer them." Ruby reached over and touched his hand, which was still atop Dog's head, and for the briefest instant, she could've sworn she saw flickers of flame appear in Preacher Wil's eyes. "You belong with us," she repeated.

"You belong with your family."

She drew her hand away, placing it back into her pocket and onto the baseball. It was warm once again, like it had been during the game against the Chicago Nine.

"Preacher Wil," Ruby said, "my daddy used to tell me we should always try to help ourselves, rather than wait for others to help us."

"Your daddy sounds like a very wise man."

"That's why I came looking for you." She brushed her hair from her eyes.

Preacher Wil sighed. "Angel, I must take you back."

"I know." She knelt to Dog and let him lick her again. Then Ruby looked up. "The Travelin' Nine need you, Preacher Wil. Come to Minneapolis."

1

★

From Ruby's Journal

Two days later . . .

I've spent most of this train ride to Minneapolis by myself. I've barely spoken a word. All the barnstormers want to talk to me, but I can't.

I don't think I'll ever be able to forgive myself for putting them through such an ordeal. I knew my disappearing would upset everyone, but I didn't realize how much. Their reactions frightened me. Mom looked as distraught as she had at Daddy's funeral, and Graham cried, though I'm not sure if that was because of me or because Mom was so unhappy. The Professor lectured me for almost an hour, telling me how selfish and inconsiderate my actions had been (like I didn't know). Then I had to hear it from Doc and Woody, too. Crazy Feet just kept shaking his head at me, and in some ways, that was even more difficult to stomach than all the talking to.

Scribe was the only one who didn't make me feel worse. He sat with me for hours, keeping me company. He didn't say much (Scribe never does), but his quiet friendship comforted me and helped me worry a little less.

Still, I couldn't help worrying about Griffith. The way he reacted was the worst of all. Griffith yelled at me, and he never yells at anyone. Ever.

But then I learned why he yelled.

Griffith and the Chancellor

Back in Chicago, Griffith met the Chancellor on the street outside our inn in the middle of the night (just writing those words terrifies me).

Facts

- The Chancellor is after the baseball.
- The Chancellor knew Griffith's name.

The Chancellor's Words

- "That's not all I want. You have something else that I want too."
- "I have something *you* want."
- "In fact, I have *more* than one thing you want."

Questions

- How did the Chancellor find out about our baseball?
- What *things* could the Chancellor possibly have that we want?
- How does the Chancellor know Griffith by name?

Theories

- Graham is somehow connected to everything that is happening.

- The Chancellor has kidnapped Uncle Owen. It explains what the Chancellor said and why Uncle Owen's warning letter arrived tattered and covered in blood.
- The Chancellor learned about the baseball from one of his men, or from Uncle Owen, or even possibly from one of the Travelin' Nine (writing those words terrifies me too).
- The Chancellor could be bluffing or setting a trap when he says he has more than one thing we want.

Our baseball causes magical things to happen during the games, but we've only begun to figure out how it works. We have a feeling it's even more powerful than we realize. We're also beginning to think that one or more of the Travelin' Nine may suspect we have it. How could they not?

Preacher Wil

I had to go back for Preacher Wil. He belongs with us, and I'm going to prove it to everyone. I'm not sure how, but I will.

I must.

He's in the next car. He's not allowed to ride in the same car with us because whites and blacks have to travel in separate cars. I don't understand rules like that.

But he is on this train to Minneapolis. Preacher Wil said that he and Dog were drifters, and they were looking for a next destination, and Minneapolis seemed as fine a city as any. He realizes there's a good chance he won't play. Not all the Travelin' Nine want him on the squad, and once we arrive in the Mill City the team is going to search for a player. Still, everyone likes Preacher Wil. The barnstormers got to know him during the two days we were delayed in Chicago.

<u>Should Preacher Wil Play for the Travelin' Nine?</u>

<u>Should</u>

Mom (Guy)

Scribe

Happy

<u>Shouldn't Because He's Not a Rough Rider</u>

Doc Lindy

Bubbles

Crazy Feet

<u>Shouldn't Because He's Black</u>

Woody

Tales

Professor Lance

<u>Dog</u>

Dog gives me hope. Preacher Wil says Dog is the best judge of character there is. He can spot a good person from a mile away.

The Travelin' Nine have taken to Dog. It helps that Dog greets each one of them with a wagging tail and a smile. Well, it looks like a smile to me. They all pat him on the head like they are rubbing him for good luck, and then Dog tilts his head to the side so they'll scratch behind his floppy left ear. He purrs like a kitten when they find his favorite spot.

Griffith spends more time with Dog than anyone. They're almost inseparable, and Preacher Wil doesn't seem to mind. I think he even likes it. I know I do. Without Dog, Griffith would probably still be yelling at me.

I've never heard Dog bark. Preacher Wil claims he does, but only on rare occasions, and when he does, Preacher Wil says you can hear it from behind a closed door, over a train engine, or from across a field of cotton.

I'm the reason why we missed the train to Minneapolis and why we had to wait two full days for the next one we all could fit on. Originally, the Rough Riders had hoped to play the game against the Lakers on Sunday because bigger crowds come out to the matches on weekends. For a while it looked like I had prevented that.

MATCH: *baseball game or contest.*

But I didn't. The torrential rains did. I was never so glad to see everything flooded and waterlogged. It's still overcast, but the rains appear to be done, and the match has been rescheduled for Tuesday. The weather made that unavoidable.

But all the heartache and pain I caused was avoidable. It's also unforgivable.

2

★

The Graham Payne Way

Extra! Extra! Read all about it!" Graham announced. He stood on the base of the lamppost, whirling around and waving the flyers. "The Lakers stink!"

"Grammy!" shouted Griffith, sidestepping through the people in the plaza.

After several days of rain, it seemed as though everyone in the Mill City was outdoors. Even though it was still cool and damp, the worst of the weather was clearly done.

"The Lakers stink!"

"The Lakers stink!" Graham repeated. "The Travelin' Nine will destroy them on Tuesday!"

"Graham Payne!" Ruby charged over.

Graham continued to swing around the post. "Come watch them get beat!"

"That's enough!" Griffith swiped at his legs. "Get down!"

"Witness the whuppin' for yourself!" Graham hopped away from his brother's grabs.

By now a crowd had gathered, and many appeared to be irritated by the little boy with the big mouth.

Griffith glanced at Scribe. It had been Griffith's idea for the Travelin' Nine's mountain of a man to accompany them to promote the game. With his intimidating presence, there would be little chance the Chancellor or his henchmen would attempt anything. However, Scribe couldn't stand too close because he might inadvertently scare people off. At the moment, Griffith could see that the barnstormers' center scout was beginning to work his way over. Surely Scribe had heard Graham and was coming to put a stop to the antics.

"This is your last warning!" Griffith yelled, fixing his glare back on his brother and pointing him to the pavement. "Get down!"

SCOUT: *outfielder. The right fielder was called the "right scout," the center fielder was called the "center scout," and the left fielder was called the "left scout."*

Graham sighed. "I'm just trying to get everyone's attention. I don't mean what I'm saying or—"

Griffith leaped into the air, yanked on Graham's pant leg, and pulled him from the post. "You can't behave like this," he lectured with a finger in his brother's face. "It's inappropriate."

"Give me one of those!" a man barked, snatching a flyer from Graham's hand.

"I want one too," a woman hollered.

Graham flashed his mischievous smile at his brother and sister. "Now what do you two have to say for yourself?" he said as he politely distributed the flyers. "It looks like the Graham Payne way is working just fine."

"It might be working," said Ruby, "but it's not right. If that's what it takes to get people to watch the Travelin' Nine, then it's not worth it."

"I'll say it's not worth it," Scribe agreed, having reached the three Paynes. He looked down at his charges. "I heard some of what was going on, and I must say, I'm most disappointed."

"No child should ever be allowed to be so disrespectful," yelled a woman standing behind Scribe.

"Where did he learn his manners?" asked another.

"My friends," Scribe said, addressing the dozens who now surrounded them. "I would like to apologize for this young man's behavior. I will see to it that—"

"We want to hear *him* apologize!" another woman interrupted.

"You're right," said Scribe. He placed a firm hand on Graham's shoulder. "I believe you have something to tell these fine folks."

Graham scrunched his face into a knot. "Fine," he said, swatting his leg with the flyers. He hopped back onto the lamppost and looked into the sea of people. "I'm sorry."

"For what?" Griffith asked, a hint of a smirk on his face.

Graham growled at his brother and then faced the crowd again. "I'm sorry for saying the things I did. I should know better. I'll never do it again." He jumped down and glared at Griffith and Ruby. "You happy now?"

"Almost," Ruby replied, leaping onto the post.

"What are you doing?" asked Graham.

"Please don't hold my brother's behavior against *us*." She spoke to the masses and held out the flyers. "Please take one. Please come to our game."

A man reached up.

Followed by a second.

Then a woman took a flyer.

And still another man.

Suddenly, Ruby couldn't pass the flyers out fast enough, and when Griffith saw what was happening, he joined his sister on the lamppost.

"I've heard of these fellas," a man said, reading the flyer. "They just beat the Chicago Nine."

"That's right, sir," Griffith said.

"Heard they played a mighty good game in Louisville," said another.

"They sure did." Ruby couldn't contain her smile. "They're terrific ballists."

"Come see for yourself how well they play," added Griffith.

"We'll be there," said yet another.

• • •

"The plan worked!" Graham exclaimed when they reached the walkway at the edge of the plaza.

"Better than I ever imagined," Ruby agreed. "Do you think anyone had any idea?"

"Not with how well I can act!" declared Griffith, inflating his chest.

"You?" Graham dismissed his brother with a wave of the hand. "That was all me. I have a future on the stage!"

"What are you three talking about?" Scribe asked.

The Payne siblings fell silent.

"What worked?" Scribe pressed. "What plan?"

Ruby sighed deeply and then gazed up at Scribe. "Graham really wasn't misbehaving. He was acting. We all were."

"I'm not sure I understand." Scribe placed his oversize hand on his chin. "I'm not sure I want to either."

"We planned all that," Griffith explained. "We thought more people would take flyers."

"It worked like a charm!" added Graham.

Scribe shook his head. "It may have worked, but it wasn't particularly honest."

"We weren't hurting anyone," Griffith contended.

"It was deceitful," Scribe maintained. "You were duping people."

Ruby suddenly felt awful. She had been inconsiderate yet again. And this time of Scribe, the one person who had stood by her on the train.

She turned away. In the distance Ruby could see the factories and warehouses lining the Minneapolis riverfront. She spotted the enormous Washburn Mill, which stood next to the field where the other members of the Travelin' Nine were practicing at this very moment. Her frown deepened. Ruby knew how much Scribe valued practicing with his fellow Rough Riders. It had taken a great deal of coaxing to get him to skip practice and chaperone their excursion instead. He didn't deserve to be treated with such disrespect.

Griffith reached up and rested a hand on Scribe's shoulder. "Did you see the way they'd heard of the Travelin' Nine?" he asked.

"Indeed I did," Scribe answered, a hint of a smile returning to his face.

"It wasn't just one person this time," Ruby added. "It was a lot of people."

"It sure was." Scribe gathered the three children closer. "That's something to always keep in mind. When you're out here promoting the Travelin' Nine, you represent them. You're the face of the team."

"And with a face like this," said Graham, "there's no stopping us!"

Scribe smiled again. "Well, now that you're almost eight, you're old enough to know—"

"Saturday's my big day," Graham interrupted with a raised arm and fist. "I can't wait. I have a huge birthday wish."

"What's the wish?" asked Ruby.

"I'm not telling," Graham replied. "If I did, it wouldn't come true. But I will say this much." He pointed at Griffith and Ruby. "Everyone is going to be so happy when it comes true. I guarantee it."

NICOLLET PARK

THE NEW HOME OF THE 1896 WESTERN LEAGUE

CHAMPION MINNEAPOLIS MILLERS

"SPACIOUS AND SPECTACULAR."

—MINNEAPOLIS TIMES

"NOTHING LIKE OLD ATHLETIC PARK, THE OLD BANDBOX BEHIND THE WEST HOTEL."

—MINNEAPOLIS JOURNAL

"A STATE-OF-THE-ART STADIUM FOR THE TWENTIETH CENTURY."

—MINNEAPOLIS TRIBUNE

If you've yet to visit Nicollet Park, what are you waiting for?

The baseballing Rough Riders' tour across the states continues. They've traveled from

Cincinnati to Louisville to Chicago and now to . . . **THE MILL CITY**

TUESDAY, AUGUST 22, 1899—12:00 P.M.

~~SUNDAY, AUGUST 20, 1899—2:00 P.M.~~

Minneapolis Lakers

versus

the Travelin' Nine

General Admission Seating: **40 cents**

Special Field-Level Box Seating: **75 cents**

3

★

Dog and Griffith

Ready, boy?" Griffith said, waving the stick in front of Dog's long snoot. "Go get!"

Griffith flinched, pretending to launch the object across the empty lawn in front of the dormitories. Dog immediately bolted off, but as soon as he realized the stick hadn't left Griffith's hand, he scampered back. Several times Griffith had faked the throw, and each time Dog had jumped the gun.

"You need to wait!" said Griffith.

Dog shook with anticipation, and the water in his coat from the wet grass sprayed about.

At last Griffith flung the stick, and Dog gave chase, following the stick's end-over-end flight as he bolted across the quadrangle. The moment it landed, Dog pounced on it with his oversize paws. He skidded to a stop, gobbled it up, and then tore back, dropping the stick at Griffith's feet.

"Good boy," Griffith declared.

He reached down to Dog, who sat up tall against Griffith's leg, and scratched behind his floppy ears. Then Griffith knelt and wrapped his arms around his new friend's torso. For such a scrappy and weathered old hound, Dog was muscled and toned.

As he picked up the stick, Griffith stole a glance at the clock atop the university library across the quad. He knew he should've already joined the others in the cafeteria for dinner, but he was having too much fun with Dog.

"Ball or stick?" Griffith asked, pulling from his pocket an old baseball that the Travelin' Nine had discarded. He held out both objects.

With a tilt of the head and a bob of the snout, Dog requested the ball. Preacher Wil had told Griffith that Dog never asked for much; the most he ever wanted was for someone to play with him.

ROCK: baseball. Also called "pill" (see below) or "rawhide" (see page 31).

Griffith dangled the rock above Dog's head and then threw it as far as he could. Dog sped off.

PILL: baseball. Also called "rock" (see above) or "rawhide" (see page 31).

But as Dog became smaller and smaller chasing after the pill, a chill surged through Griffith. He realized just how vulnerable he was on the empty quad. The last time he'd been alone outdoors, he'd encountered the Chancellor.

When Dog finally reached the ball and began bounding back across the grounds,

Griffith relaxed his tense shoulders and exhaled a long breath. As Dog approached, he began to prance with his tail held high. He shook the rawhide proudly in his jaws, before dropping it into Griffith's cupped hand.

"Attaboy," Griffith said, grabbing Dog's nose and playfully shaking it. "One more?"

Dog bobbed his head and backed away.

"Let's see if you can catch this one," said Griffith. "Fetch!"

This time, Griffith didn't throw the ball far. Instead, he threw it high, as high as he could. Dog circled under the pill like an accomplished outfielder and snared it in his mouth.

"Great catch, Dog!" Griffith cheered. "You could play for the Travelin' Nine!"

RAWHIDE: *baseball. Also called "pill" or "rock" (see page 30).*

Dog sat across the room in front of the partially open door. He was on guard. No one would be entering without his permission.

"Great catch, Dog!"

"Not only is that drifter dog an impeccable judge of character," Preacher Wil had told Griffith and Ruby, "but he is also fiercely protective."

Preacher Wil was right. At the slightest sound—the tree limb against the windowpane above Ruby's bed or Graham's soft snoring—Dog's ears would perk up.

Griffith lifted his head off his pillow and looked over at his brother and sister, sleeping soundly in their beds. At dinner, Preacher Wil had offered to let Dog stay the night with them in their dorm room. It was almost as if Preacher Wil had known that something had spooked Griffith, and that Griffith needed Dog near him.

Peering across at Dog, a hint of a smile crept onto Griffith's face. For the first time, he realized that there seemed to be a little bit of each of the Travelin' Nine in Dog. His grayish-white coat brought to mind Happy, and the black markings around his eye resembled the Professor's patch. The way Dog sprinted across the quad reminded Griffith of how Crazy Feet pursued a star chaser. And since Dog didn't bark, he was a dog of few words, like Scribe was a man of few words.

STAR CHASER: *fly ball to the outfield, or "outer garden" (see page 49). Also sometimes referred to as "cloud hunter" (see page 84) or "sky ball" (see page 84).*

Even in the darkness, Griffith could see that Dog was watching him, waiting for a command. So Griffith gave one—an ever-so-slight lifting of his chin. Dog sprang to his paws and walked softly across the room. When he reached Griffith's bed, he sat down, stared up at Griffith, and waited again.

Griffith blinked his eyes and tilted his head. Then Dog took several steps back, turned two circles, and leaped onto the bed. He lay alongside Griffith, nudging him with his long nose as if he were telling Griffith to scoot over.

So Griffith did.

Both boy and dog were sound asleep.

Dog seemed to smile, but his expression said something more. It appeared to say that he understood about tomorrow's meeting, the one where the Travelin' Nine would determine whether or not Preacher Wil would be permitted to play.

The meeting was the reason why Griffith couldn't sleep. It was all he could think about. But in a way, he was relieved. The meeting kept him from thinking about Ruby disappearing back in Chicago and how he had thought he might never see his sister again. It also kept him from thinking about the Chancellor.

He looked down at Dog, who exhaled an exaggerated sigh and shut his eyes. His floppy ears dangled forward like an extra pair of lids. Griffith rested his hand on Dog's belly and felt it rise and fall with each breath.

In a matter of moments, both boy and dog were sound asleep.

4

★

Meeting of the Minds

he Travelin' Nine sat in a circle in the middle of the empty library. They had the space all to themselves this morning. In exchange for a couple of box seats to the match, the head librarian was allowing the barnstormers to use the facility until it opened to the public at noon.

"We've come together again to make a critical decision," the Professor said, standing in the center as he presided over the meeting. "However, this time, more than likely, we will not all be in agreement."

Ruby chewed on her bottom lip and peered nervously around at the Rough Riders. She hated it when they disagreed about anything, and she certainly wished they weren't disagreeing over Preacher Wil.

What if they vote against him? What if they don't allow him to play?

Yesterday's dreary weather had been less than ideal for baseball tryouts. Only a few prospects had shown up at practice, and none had been worthy of consideration. The Travelin' Nine had been unable to secure a replacement ballist, and now, with time running short, they had to decide whether to play shorthanded or allow Preacher Wil to join the team.

Ruby gazed around the room. She had never been in a library quite like this. The ones back home all resembled her classroom at school, but this one was built vertically, standing three stories tall. Circular in shape, its rounded walls were filled with books. Rolling ladders attached to the beams below the ceiling were used to reach the upper shelves. For a library, it was dimly lit. The empty candleholders affixed to the top and sides of the card catalogs looked like they hadn't been used in ages. The only source of light this morning filtered through the small, octagonal windows evenly spaced among the bookcases.

CRANKS: *fans, usually the hometown fans. Also called "rooters" (see page 40).*

Gripping the baseball in her pocket, she looked at her brothers, side by side across the circle. Griffith and Graham weren't in chairs like the others; they sat on one of the tables that had been pushed to the side for the meeting. Griffith wore a long face, and every few minutes, he would rub his eyes with his palms.

"We have to face reality," Professor Lance stated. "Preacher Wil's skin color could be an issue."

"I reckon some of the cranks may say

awful things," added Woody. "Or worse yet, they may decide not to attend. We can't afford that. We need as many rooters at this game as possible."

"What if the Lakers refuse to play?" Tales asked. "What if the umpire refuses to officiate?"

"He could make calls against us," Woody noted.

ROOTERS: *fans; people who cheer at ball games. Also called "cranks"* *(see page 39).*

The Professor nodded. "Sadly, those are all distinct possibilities. That's why I think it will be too costly to have Preacher Wil play. If we play with only eight ballists, at least we have a chance."

"I want it to be perfectly clear," Tales added, twitching his bushy mustache, "I have absolutely no problem with Preacher Wil's skin color. I don't believe the Professor and Woody have an issue with his race either. It's the reactions of others that have us worried."

"What's wrong with the color of Preacher Wil's skin?" asked Graham, hopping off the table and entering the circle. "My daddy always used to tell us there was only one race: the human race."

"I reckon that's what Guy used to say to us," Woody noted. "In Cuba, men of all walks of life fought shoulder to shoulder."

"The color of one's skin shouldn't make a difference," said Tales, "but in 1899, I'm afraid that it does."

"I'm afraid it still may in 1999 and 2099," Professor Lance added. He took Graham's seat on the table.

"Then we'll just have to change the way people think," Graham said.

Elizabeth smiled a proud smile. "I wish it were that easy."

Ruby glanced to Preacher Wil and saw that both his fists were tightly clenched. Preacher Wil never kept his right hand balled up, only his left, which he liked to tuck behind his back or otherwise hide from plain view. She wished Preacher Wil's rugged right hand was open and welcoming like it usually was.

He sat in the circle with the rest of the ballists, his eyes darting from voice to voice. Preacher Wil had asked to be here. He had wanted to hear what the Travelin' Nine had to say, and none of the players had objected. So far, he hadn't uttered a word, and his stoic expression told Ruby he would more than likely remain silent.

"It's not just Preacher Wil's skin color that's an issue," Bubbles spoke up. "He's not a Rough Rider. He wasn't with us in Cuba. That's why I object to his playing."

"That's my position as well," agreed Doc Lindy. "It's why I opposed auditioning players at practice."

Crazy Feet nodded.

"I wish there were other baseball-playing

Rough Riders, but there aren't," Bubbles said, scratching what remained of his left ear. "If we play with someone who isn't a Rough Rider, do we even know if the magical events will occur?"

"Well, those of us who practiced yesterday," Elizabeth chimed in, "all saw how well Preacher Wil can play."

Ruby looked at Preacher Wil again. The barnstormers had made no secret of how impressed they had been with Preacher Wil's ball-playing abilities. He had thrown part of batting practice, exhibiting excellent control as well as lively movement on his pitches. At the plate, he'd demonstrated he could hit to all fields.

"Magic or no magic," Elizabeth continued, "I for one believe we'll have a better chance with nine ballists than with eight."

"Everyone has made valid arguments here this morning," Professor Lance said, standing back up. "But unfortunately, we've run out of time." He pointed to his watch. "The library will be opening shortly. We must end the debate and hold our vote. When I ask for hands, only those in favor of Preacher Wil playing should raise them."

Ruby looked around the circle. She bit down on her lip even harder than before. This was the moment.

Be together. Always.

Uncle Owen's words echoed in Ruby's mind. She pressed her palm to her forehead. No matter the outcome, the Rough Riders weren't together, and in her heart, she knew that was a problem. A *big* problem. She slipped her hand back into her pocket.

Please vote for him. Please let him play.

"If you feel Preacher Wil should be allowed to play," Professor Lance said, "raise your hand now."

Elizabeth, Happy, and Scribe raised their hands right away.

Please vote for him.

"Well, I still wish we could somehow find us another Rough Rider," said Bubbles, slowly raising his hand, "but I also believe we'll be better off if we field a full squad."

Then Crazy Feet raised his hand, followed by Doc Lindy.

"Six votes!" Ruby exclaimed, leaping off her chair. "Preacher Wil plays!"

5

★

A Sudden Change of Plan

eaning over the iron bridge's guardrail, Graham finally had a clear view of St. Anthony Falls.

"It looks exactly like it did in the pamphlet," he said to Griffith.

On the train ride north, the attendant had given Graham an *In the Land of 10,000 Lakes* pamphlet. The Minnesota brochure had a separate section devoted to the only naturally occurring waterfall on the entire Mississippi River, and Graham had read all of it to Griffith.

At the moment, however, Griffith had little interest in the river or the falls. Walking alongside his siblings and the barnstormers as they headed to the trolley that would take them down to Lake Street and Nicollet Park, something felt amiss. In his cupped hands, he squeezed the baseball he had used to play catch with Dog.

The Chancellor was up to something. They were walking into a trap. Griffith had no idea what the Chancellor had in store for them, but he was sure—

"Hello!" Graham said, knocking on Griffith's head. "Anyone home?"

Griffith ducked away and smiled. "I'm here," he replied.

"I hope so," said Graham. "In a little while, we'll be at the stadium."

"I heard it's a lot like League Park," Ruby said, alluding to the field they had visited back in Cincinnati. She slid between her brothers. "It has a big scoreboard, real dugouts, billboards along the outer garden fence, and rows and rows of bleachers. It's supposed to be the most beautiful stadium in the entire state."

Like a platoon heading for battle, the barnstormers marched down Blaisdell Avenue. For most of the way from the trolley, they had walked in four tight rows, but now, as they approached the corner, the players parted for Dog. The canine wanted to be in front. His floppy ears had perked up, and he had begun to growl softly.

OUTER GARDEN: *outfield. The outfield was once known as the garden. So left field was called "left garden," center field was referred to as "center garden," and right field was known as "right garden."*

As soon as the team turned the corner onto the plaza leading into Nicollet Park, the veterans understood why. Before them stood a line of men, ballists in uniform, silent and tall. As the Travelin' Nine approached, one man stepped forward. He appeared to be the oldest of the bunch. He held a sheet of paper in his hand.

"The name's Wilmot," the man said. "Walter Wilmot. I'm the right scout and the manager of the Millers. The Minneapolis Millers."

"We're scheduled to play the Lakers," Happy declared, stepping up. "Are they already inside the stadium?"

Wilmot shook his head. "We're your opponents today. Here's the lineup you'll be facing." He passed the paper to Happy.

"I don't think I understand." Happy took the sheet, glanced at it, and then handed it to Professor Lance.

Griffith felt his chest begin to tighten as he peeked at the names on the sheet in the Professor's hands.

1. **Germany Smith**
2. **Jay Andrews**
3. **Roger Bresnahan**
4. **Jack Menefee**
5. **Perry Werden**
6. **Ed Abbatichie**
7. **Walter Wilmot**
8. **Wee Willie "Doc" Nance**
9. **Kid McNeely**

The Minneapolis Millers were professional ballists in the Western League, and this season they were only a few games out of first place. Griffith swallowed hard. How could the Travelin' Nine possibly compete against a pro team? And why would the Lakers agree to the last-minute switch?

He gazed down the row of Rough Riders and across at the line of Millers. Separated by only a few yards, the ballists from both squads were assuming more menacing postures and poses.

HURLER: *pitcher.*

"Why the sudden change in plans?" Happy asked.

Wilmot shook his head again but didn't say a word. He slid back into line with the rest of his players.

"What happened to the Lakers?" The Professor stepped forward and stood next to Happy. "Does this have something to do with our hurler's skin color?"

Griffith swallowed hard.

"This is our house," Wilmot stated flatly. He motioned with his thumb to the stadium behind him. "Ever since we left Athletic Park two years ago for this magnificent shrine, we've been the only hosts. For as long as I'm manager, it's going to stay that way."

"We had specific arrangements with the Lakers," Happy protested. "We agreed to split all the money from tickets and gave—"

"That's also been revised," Wilmot interrupted. "This contest is now winner take all."

"That's not what—"

"This is not a negotiation," Wilmot cut Happy off again. "The Millers are a team of professionals. This is how we do business. We're not some second-rate squad like the Lakers. Nor are we like those cheap ballists who play across the river."

Griffith knew Wilmot was referring to the St. Paul Saints, the nearby baseball club whose owner was so cheap he made his ballists play in their dirty socks.

Happy sighed. "We'll provide you with our lineup at the field." With a new ballist on the team, they'd decided to mix the batting order up a bit but didn't have a revised roster in hand.

"So you are accepting these terms?" Wilmot asked.

"It looks like we don't have an alternative."

Wilmot smiled. Then he crossed his arms and looked to Griffith, Ruby, and Graham. "Of course, only uniformed players are permitted in the dugout."

"Now see here." Woody stepped forward. "I reckon I've heard enough—"

"No, Woody." Happy blocked his way with an outstretched arm and gently guided him back into the row. "We're accepting their terms." Happy then turned back to Wilmot. "What about dogs?"

Wilmot scratched his chin. "I have no

problem with a hound in the dugout." He nodded to Dog. "I'm a dog man myself. Children, however, are completely different animals."

"We can't allow this to happen." Elizabeth's voice trembled as she spoke to the group.

"What choice do we have?" asked Tales.

Elizabeth shook her head. "They can't be by themselves in this stadium. This is horrible. Not with . . ." Her voice trailed off.

Griffith looked away. At the far end of the plaza, Wilmot and the rest of the Millers were entering Nicollet Park. As they disappeared into the stadium, Griffith's mind raced full speed ahead. But for the first time all day, there was a *clarity* to his thoughts.

The Chancellor had orchestrated this switch. The Chancellor was the reason the Travelin' Nine would now be playing a professional opponent. The Chancellor was also

"We can't allow this to happen."

the reason he and his sister and brother weren't permitted in the dugout. If they were separated from the adults, he could get the baseball and whatever else he wanted. Griffith had suspected the Chancellor would try some trickery. He'd been right.

"What are we going to do, Griff?" Ruby whispered to her brother, while the adults discussed the situation.

"We'll watch the game from the grandstand," Griffith replied confidently. "We'll be like all the other cranks."

"But don't you see what's happening?" Ruby clutched her journal to her chest. "He's after us."

"I know he is," Griffith said. "We'll keep moving around. We'll be fine."

"How can you say that?" asked Ruby, slipping her other hand into her pocket and teasing the baseball's stitching with her fingertips. "Maybe Happy should stay with us."

But even as she made the suggestion, Ruby realized that wasn't possible. At the moment, Happy stood to her right with his head bowed and his nine fingers over his face. The trip to the stadium had exhausted him. Happy was far too ill to be running around.

"Take Dog with you," Elizabeth said, walking over.

Griffith thought for a moment. It wasn't a bad idea. Dog could be a deterrent; he could help keep the Chancellor's men away. But if anything were to happen to Dog, Griffith would never forgive himself.

"No," Griffith replied. "Mom, we'll be fine. I'll take care of Ruby and Graham."

"You're going to take care of me?" Graham pointed to himself and laughed. "I'd like to see that!"

"Well, you're going to see that," Griffith stated so firmly that Graham's grin disappeared.

Griffith glanced down at Dog, who had walked up beside him and nudged his hand.

"We'll be fine." Griffith looked his mother in the eye.

"I want you to stay as close to the dugout as possible," Elizabeth instructed. She spoke quickly. "Make sure you're always in plain view, and if anyone tries to—"

"I'll make sure of it," Griffith interrupted. He reached over and held her arm. "I promise."

Elizabeth placed her hand atop Griffith's and squeezed. Then she managed a smile and let go.

Peering up at the stadium, Griffith ran his hands through his thick hair. He was going to have to outwit the Chancellor. But as frightened as he should have been, he wasn't. Instead he was angry. Griffith wouldn't allow anyone to hurt his family. Even if that meant facing down the Chancellor himself.

He was going to have to outwit the Chancellor.

Still, there was one thing that Griffith found terribly troubling. How was it that the Chancellor managed to be one step ahead of them? It was almost as if the Chancellor himself or one of his men were traveling with the barnstormers. It didn't make sense.

"Maybe we'll find a way to sneak into the dugout," Graham said to Ruby and Griffith.

"Maybe," Ruby tried to assure him. She looked to their mother, who was now back with the other ballists and walking toward the stadium.

"We'll figure it out," said Griffith. He placed a steady hand on his brother's shoulder. "Just remember what Dad always said to us."

"You mean what we talked about after the game in Cincinnati?" Graham asked as they trailed after the barnstormers.

Ruby nodded and began to repeat their father's words. "We often can't control what happens to us . . ."

". . . but what we can control is how we deal with it," Graham finished the phrase.

"You got it," said Griffith, squeezing his brother's shoulder.

Then Griffith turned around. When he did, he saw something he had hoped he wouldn't, but had known he would. More than a dozen men, all wearing finely tailored suits with pink pocket squares in their breast pockets, were following them into Nicollet Park.

6

★

The Direct Threat

One by one, the Travelin' Nine emerged from the dugout beyond the third base line and took the field for pregame practice.

CUT: *swing.*

RUBBER: *pitching strip on the mound. The pitcher must have one foot touching the rubber when pitching.*

Graham lowered his chin to his chest. The barnstormers had told him he could still take his good-luck cut even with Happy no longer toeing the rubber. However, that had changed when the Millers greeted them in the plaza. All Graham could do now was watch from the middle of the narrow aisle in the stands.

He glanced back at his brother standing in the row behind him. Griffith wasn't watching the field; he was preoccupied with the people walking the runways and filling the benches.

"Two more minutes," Griffith said without turning around. "Then we need to find a safer spot."

Graham groaned. "I heard you the first fifty times."

"It was only forty-eight."

"Knowing you, you probably counted."

While the sun still hadn't broken through the clouds, the cool overcast had been replaced by warmer temperatures. It was now sticky and muggy. Griffith pumped a fist as he watched more and more cranks pour into the bleachers. With so many in attendance and with some seats costing as much as seventy-five cents, if the Travelin' Nine

This game was not going to be easy.

could somehow find a way to win the match, they would raise hundreds of dollars. Such a large sum of money would go a long way toward helping to pay off Uncle Owen's ten-thousand-dollar debt.

But Griffith realized that finding a way to win this game was not going to be easy.

Looking down the stands, Griffith noted that ushers stood at the top or bottom of every aisle that led to the field. He stared intently up at the man in the next aisle. Something about him seemed familiar, but he couldn't quite figure out what it was. Then he peeked over at the attendant by the dugout and saw the large scar running along his hand. Suddenly Griffith understood why they looked familiar. Some of these ushers were actually the Chancellor's thugs in disguise. One he had seen on the train to Chicago and another had been with the Chancellor in the Windy City.

He squeezed the back of his neck and

looked to Ruby. She sat on a still-empty bench several feet over, nervously tapping her journal. Her eyes darted from the bleachers to the field to Graham.

Like Griffith, Ruby understood that it wasn't safe for them to stay in one spot for long. She had volunteered to be in charge of finding different places where they could watch the game.

"We need to get moving," Griffith said. "Have you figured out where we'll be for the first frame?"

FRAME: *inning.*

"Far from here," answered Ruby. She pointed toward the wooden wall beyond left garden. "It looks like there may be an alcove back there."

"We won't be able to see a thing," Graham complained.

"You're looking at it all wrong," Ruby said. "You'll see the action exactly like Crazy Feet and Scribe."

"We should be safe out there," Griffith agreed, "but we can only stay for an inning. Two at most. Then we'll have to find a new spot."

"I'm already working on that."

With Griffith watching out for the Chancellor's men, Ruby led her brothers around and through Nicollet Park. Wandering the bleachers, she noticed that some of the benches farthest from the field were located behind rafters or directly in back of pillars. She wondered if the cranks stuck in those seats had to pay full price. And since the wooden benches were unbearably hard, she couldn't imagine how anyone managed to stay seated for a whole game. Dozens and dozens of vendors filled the aisles. She was impressed by how easily they squeezed through the narrow laneways while holding their trays of beverages and snacks. If only they were giving away the treats like they had back in Chicago, she thought.

As they approached the stands beyond the left garden foul pole, Ruby glanced at the ballists. The players on the pitch were *below* the cranks; every seat in the house was elevated. The rooters in the front row could stand up, lean over the railing, and, if a ballist approached, rest their hands atop his cap. They could also . . .

PITCH: *playing field. Also called "green oasis" (see page 71).*

"Hold it right there!"

Griffith, Ruby, and Graham whirled around.

A man raced up from behind. A second one charged down a runway. A third approached them from the side. Two wore finely pressed suits with pink pocket squares. One wore an usher's uniform.

Griffith instinctively jumped in front of his brother, while Ruby's hand automatically reached into her pocket. She pressed the baseball to her hip.

"Give us that ball!" one of the men ordered. "Now!"

"What ball?" Graham fired back.

"Leave us alone," said Griffith.

"Looks like we have a wise guy over here," the man in the usher's uniform snickered. He leaned over and pointed down at Graham. "You know what we like to do with wise guys. We—"

"I said, leave us alone," Griffith repeated.

"I'll scream," Ruby added, inching closer to Griffith so that their shoulders brushed, and they formed a wall in front of Graham.

"Go ahead," the third thug replied. "Scream. See what happens. Do you really think any of *these* ushers will come to your aid?"

Griffith gulped. They were trapped. He pressed a hand to his side, and that was when he remembered he still had something.

"You want our baseball?" Griffith suddenly said. "Fine, you can have it. But once we give it to you, you're going to leave our family alone."

"What are you doing, Griff?" asked Graham, tugging his brother's arm. "Don't!"

The man who had pointed down at Graham now directed his finger at Griffith's eyes. "We decide when to leave someone alone," he said. "No one orders us around."

"Well, this time someone does," Griffith barked back, surprised by the power and force of his words.

"We're not asking for that ball," the man said. He leaned in so close that his face hovered over Griffith's. "We're demanding it."

"You want it?" Griffith reached into his pocket and pulled out a baseball. "Fine. Fetch!" He wagged the rawhide in the man's face and then launched it into the

"Fetch!"

bleachers between third sack and home dish.

"No!" Graham yelled.

The three henchmen instantly took off.

"Run!" shouted Griffith, pointing his brother and sister toward the outer garden.

"My ball!" Graham screamed. "My ball!"

"Go!" Griffith ordered.

Ruby charged off, leading them around the foul pole and into the area beyond the outer garden wall. They raced down the steps toward the field, then quickly ducked into the alcove tucked under the first few rows of seats, the alcove she had pointed to a short time ago.

SACK: base. Also called "bag" (see page 93).

DISH: home plate.

"That was close," she said, resting her hands on her knees as she tried to catch her breath.

"I'll say," Griffith added between pants.

"Do you think they'll realize that's not the baseball?" Ruby asked.

Graham's eyes bulged. "It's not?"

Griffith shook his head. "That was the ball I used to play catch with Dog." He then reached over and patted Ruby's pocket. "Those goons will realize that once they see the teeth marks."

Graham scrunched his face into a knot and growled like Dog.

"What is it, Grammy?" Griffith asked.

"What is it? I'll tell you what it is." He spoke through gritted teeth. "I'm tired of you two hiding things from me. What do they want from *me*?"

Ruby looked to Griffith. Neither said a word.

"Don't pretend like you don't know what I'm talking about." Graham fired daggers at his siblings. "I'm not blind and deaf. I see the way the barnstormers look at me, and I see the way you and Mom look at me. Don't you think it's time you told me what's really going on?"

Still no response.

"Why are those guys in the suits following us everywhere we go?" Graham stepped closer to his brother and sister. "Who's this 'he' person?"

Griffith had never seen Graham this angry, and a part of him wanted to tell his younger brother everything. Graham was absolutely right. He was entitled to an explanation. But Griffith wasn't sure how Graham would react to learning that the Chancellor was after them. And perhaps more importantly, Griffith had promised his mother he wouldn't say a word. If Griffith was to say anything to Graham, he needed to let her know first.

"What if I refuse to move around?" Graham continued, folding his arms tightly across his chest. "What if I want to watch the game from right behind home dish? And don't try making up some story that we need tickets or something. I'm not buying it. I'm not believing *anything* you tell me anymore."

Griffith exhaled a long breath. "Grammy, you're not wrong for feeling the way you do," he finally said. "After the game, I'm going to talk to Mom. It's time we all sat down and had a family meeting." He glanced at Ruby and then placed both hands on his brother's shoulders. "For today, we need you to stay right beside us and pay extra close attention."

"Fine," said Graham, holding up both hands, palms out. "I'll be a good sport and go along with your little game. But I'm warning you, this is the last time. Before my birthday on Saturday, I'm going to know everything that you do. And by the way, I have secrets too." He faced Ruby. "Want to hear what Scribe said about you?"

"What did he say?" she asked.

"Wouldn't you like to know?" Graham

raised a single eyebrow and smiled.

Ruby rolled her eyes. "I bet he didn't even say anything."

"Maybe he did. Maybe he didn't."

7

★

A Shaky Start

Peering through the gaps in the wooden slats of the outfield fence, Griffith, Ruby, and Graham watched the local ballists take the pitch. Since the Millers had made it perfectly clear *they* were the home team, there would be no pregame footrace this afternoon to determine which squad batted first.

GREEN OASIS: *playing field. Also called "pitch" (see page 70).*

"It's about that time again," Griffith said.

Across the green oasis, Ruby spotted Preacher Wil, sitting alone at the end of the dugout bench. She couldn't see Dog from where she stood in the small, dimly lit space,

Peering through the gaps . . .

but he was sure to be lying on Preacher Wil's boots.

What if I'm wrong? What if he doesn't belong? What if I've made things worse?

No, she told herself. She still believed with all her heart that Preacher Wil needed to be with them, and she was as determined as ever to prove it.

Without taking her eyes from the field, Ruby reached for the baseball. She wondered how they would communicate with the Travelin' Nine once things started to happen—if they did. They needed to come up with a way to relay instructions to the ballists. . . .

"Earth to Ruby," said Graham, knocking on Ruby's head like he had rapped on Griffith's a short time before. He cupped his hand over his mouth and spoke directly into her ear. "Hello! Anyone home?"

"How long were you trying to get my attention?" she asked, pulling her face from the fence.

"Long enough." Griffith smiled. "You ready?"

For the first time today, Ruby took out the baseball. All three jaws dropped instantly.

"What happened to it?" Graham asked.

"I have no idea," Ruby replied. The seams on their already weathered ball were looser than ever, and some of the stitching had frayed nearly to the point of disintegration.

"How could that be?" Graham wondered.

"I haven't done anything differently," she said. She passed the ball to Griffith.

Ruby shuddered as her older brother studied it. Their baseball was *mirroring* what was happening with the Rough Riders. When her eyes met Griffith's, she could tell he was thinking the same thing. Like the Travelin' Nine, their baseball was less together, and maybe even falling apart.

"Let's give this a shot anyway," said Griffith, passing the

ball back to Ruby and then resting his hand on top of it.

Graham added his hand to the baseball. Then Ruby inserted her pinky into the odd, acorn-size hole, and the moment she did, it started. Not a breeze this time, but rather the roar of rushing waters.

"It's working already!" Graham exclaimed.

The three Paynes pressed their faces to the fence and gazed out at the field. But all they saw was Crazy Feet stepping to the plate to lead off for the Travelin' Nine.

DAISY CUTTER: *ground ball. Also known as "grass clipper" (see page 93) or "bug bruiser" (see page 101).*

"Give it time," Griffith said. "Let's see what Crazy Feet can do."

"Start us off!" Ruby cheered.

But Crazy Feet lacked his usual patience at the plate. He swung at the first pitch and grounded a lazy daisy cutter down to first sack. Perry Werden needed to take only a half step to record the out.

Tales also showed surprisingly little plate discipline. Like Crazy Feet, he swung at Kid

McNeely's initial offering and popped an easy sky ball right to the Millers' hurler for the second out of the match.

Griffith shook his head. Why weren't the table setters taking any pitches? His father used to tell him that strikers who lacked confidence were often overly aggressive. But why would both Crazy Feet and Tales be uncertain at the plate? It made no sense.

It made even less sense when Woody took only one pitch, and then swung at a high and outside ball, lifting a routine cloud hunter to center that Jack Menafee snared for the final out of the frame.

Three batters up, three hands dead.

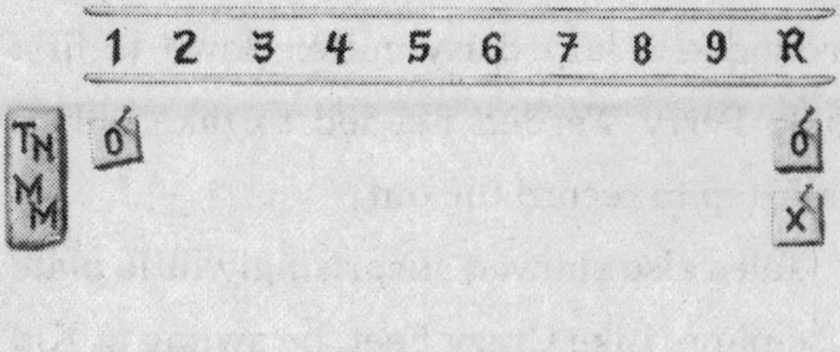

SKY BALL: *fly ball to the outfield, or "outer garden" (see page 49). Also sometimes referred to as "star chaser" (see page 34) or "cloud hunter" (see below).*

TABLE SETTERS: *Sometimes the first two batters in the lineup are called "table setters." They "set the table" for all the other strikers in the batting order by getting on base.*

STRIKER: *batter, or hitter.*

CLOUD HUNTER: *fly ball to the outfield, or "outer garden" (see page 49). Also sometimes referred to as "star chaser" (see page 34) or "sky ball" (see above).*

THREE HANDS DEAD: *three outs.*

8

★

Preacher Wil Takes the Hill

Preacher Wil reached under his collar for his necklace. He twirled the charm in his fingers and kissed it gently before tucking it back in. Then he stepped forth from the dugout, and for the first time in many, many years, he headed to the hill to pitch in a baseball game.

HILL: *pitcher's mound. Also called "bump" (see page 110).*

From half a field away, through the slats in the outfield fence, Ruby could see the pride on his face. She smiled wide.

But as Preacher Wil crossed over the foul

line and into fair territory, the raging-river sound grew louder.

"I don't like what I'm hearing," Griffith said.

Neither did Ruby. With each step Preacher Wil took toward the mound, the din of roaring rapids rose until it hit almost eardrum-piercing levels. Some of the Travelin' Nine covered their ears (though Bubbles only covered what remained of his left one). However, the Millers and their cranks didn't because they couldn't hear a thing.

FOUL LINES: *lines extending from home plate through first and third base and all the way to the outfield. Anything within the lines is considered to be in fair territory; anything outside the lines is in foul territory.*

When Preacher Wil reached the rubber, the surface of the field began to crack. Water surged in, and for a moment the pitcher's mound became an island. In a matter of seconds a chasm opened up, and the water rushed into it, slicing a divide across the entire pitch. The waterway started by the Millers' dugout, cut through the infield between Tales and second sack, and swung

Water surged in . . .

back to the outer garden wall. Professor, Tales, and Woody stood on one side of the river, while the rest of the Rough Riders were on the other.

"Look at the way it's divided the barnstormers." Ruby pointed. "The three players who voted against Preacher Wil because of his skin color are separated from the rest of the team."

"How did you see that so fast?" asked Griffith.

"That's easy, Griff," Graham answered first. "Your little sister is smarter than you!"

Griffith elbowed Graham. "And my little brother is about to get sat on!"

"Only we can see this," Ruby noted, directing her brothers' eyes to the Millers' dugout and the cranks seated behind it. None of the locals were reacting to the new on-field obstacle.

"How are the barnstormers going to play

with a river running through the field?" Graham asked.

The stream was far too wide for the ballists to hurdle, and even though it was level, the fast-moving, rushing rapids made it unsafe for swimming. If a batted ball or throw happened to land in the water, the ballists would have to wait for the currents to carry it ashore.

Ruby frowned. "I have a feeling this is just the beginning."

She faced the mound again and noticed that Preacher Wil had *transformed*. Firing his warm-up tosses to Guy, he no longer looked like the kind and gentle man she had come to know these last few days. His welcoming smile and soothing eyes had vanished. Preacher Wil now looked like a warrior.

"Good," Ruby whispered to herself. "That's exactly what the Travelin' Nine need."

• • •

Preacher Wil stared down Germany Smith, the Minneapolis Millers' leadoff striker. Then he peered in at Guy's target, dipped his left hand into his mitt, and gripped the pill. Finally he raised his arms high over his head, pivoted into his windup, and fired the first pitch.

All Smith could do was watch the perfect fastball sail right over the heart of home dish.

But the umpire failed to lift his right fist and signal a strike. Instead, both hands remained on his knees.

Griffith, Ruby, Graham, and the barnstormers wanted to question the umpire's call; however, everyone knew better than to challenge his authority. Once an umpire issued a ruling, there was never a debate.

For his next offering, Preacher Wil threw a fluttering curveball, a pitch even more perfect than his first—if that were possible. And for the second time in a row, all Germany

Smith could do was watch it cross the plate.

Yet once again, the umpire didn't rise out of his crouch behind the dish to indicate a strike.

"Where was it?" Graham asked.

"That's what I'd like to know," replied Griffith.

Graham pounded his leg with a fist. "That umpire shouldn't be wearing a top hat and tails. He should be wearing a Millers uniform."

"Daddy always told us never to disagree with an umpire," Ruby grumbled, "but it's impossible to agree with this one."

The three Paynes realized they were up against a force they had no control over. All the calls—close and not so close—were going in favor of the home team. It was like the Millers were playing with ten ballists.

Preacher Wil had to realize it too, but his mound manner didn't change.

Germany Smith took Preacher Wil's next two pitches as well, and on four straight *strikes*, the Millers had their leadoff man on.

"He can't find the plate!" a row of rooters began to chant.

"Anyone have a map?" shouted a fan. "Pitcher needs directions to the dish!"

"The southpaw needs glasses!" another chorus of cranks sang.

SOUTHPAW: *left-handed individual; the commonly used nickname for players who throw left-handed.*

And others called out even worse insults—ones that mocked Preacher Wil's skin color.

Griffith grabbed the back of his neck. Listening to the cries of the locals, he was reminded of the conversations he used to have with his father when they played catch in the yard. His father would lament how baseball had changed. It used to be a gentlemen's sport, but because it had grown rapidly, it had acquired an edge, an edge his father could not accept or understand.

In spite of the umpire's calls and the

fans' behavior, Preacher Wil didn't so much as flinch. He simply kept on pitching.

The Millers' next batter took the first two pitches, both strikes that were called balls. Ahead in the count, he swung at the third offering, grounding a grass clipper to Bubbles at shortstop, a surefire double-play ball. However, in order to cover the sack, Tales had to cross the stream. He instinctively broke for the bag, but then realized the water was in the way. Screeching to a halt, he teetered along the shore like a tightrope walker struggling to keep his balance. With Tales trying not to topple, Bubbles's only play was to first.

GRASS CLIPPER: *ground ball. Also known as "daisy cutter" (see page 83) or "bug bruiser" (see page 101).*

BAG: *base. Also called "sack" (see page 74).*

Splash!

To the Minneapolitans, it seemed like Bubbles didn't know how to force out a base runner. They had no idea what to make of Tales, either. He was lying facedown on the infield dirt, kicking his arms and legs like a

Tales had to cross the stream.

baby (though he was really battling the current). Then, when he climbed back onto dry land and began wringing out his clothes, the locals thought he had truly lost his marbles.

"We need to get rid of that river." Graham waved at the waterway. "They can't make plays."

"I don't think that river's going anywhere," Ruby stated.

"What makes you say that?" asked Graham.

"As long as the Travelin' Nine are divided," she said, shaking her head, "that field's going to be divided."

The next batter, the Millers' strapping young catcher, Roger Bresnahan, smacked a sky ball to right. Ordinarily it would have been an easy catch for Woody. However, because of what had happened on the previous play, the Travelin Nine's right scout didn't race after the rawhide. Stopping a few strides short of the stream, he waited for the splash landing. Then he plucked the ball from the water and shook it out before firing it back in to the cutoff man. By that time Germany Smith had scored from second, and the Millers had the early lead.

"Hang in there, Preacher Wil," Ruby whispered. "Hang in there."

As frustrated as she was by the unfair umpire, the unruly cranks, and the divided diamond, Ruby refused to lose hope. For one thing, the hometown hitters were swinging the timber and looking to put the ball in play. So long as they were, the Travelin' Nine had a chance to record outs.

Preacher Wil was the other reason for hope. He was more than maintaining his poise and holding his own on the hill. The next striker, Jack Menefee, skied to Scribe in center for out number two, and Bresnahan was unable to advance from second sack.

CUTOFF MAN: *infielder who catches a throw from an outfielder in an attempt to hold up a base runner who is heading for a base or home plate or to help a ball get to its intended target faster.*

DIAMOND: *infield.*

TIMBER: *baseball bat. Also called "lumber"* *(see page 110).*

SKY (v.): *to hit a fly ball.*

Then Perry Werden hit a liner up the middle that Preacher Wil plucked from the air with his bare hand to close out the frame.

"It could've been worse," Griffith noted.

"A lot worse," added Ruby.

"They only got one," Graham pointed out. "Now we need to figure out how to get that river to disappear."

All of a sudden, that's what started to occur. As Preacher Wil stepped from the hill and the players began leaving the pitch, the waters slowed and the river narrowed. By the time the Travelin' Nine had reached the dugout and the Millers had retaken the field, not a single drop of water remained.

LINER: *line-drive batted ball.*

"It's gone!" Graham announced.

"And so are we," Griffith said, letting go of the baseball.

"What do you mean?" asked Graham.

Ruby knew exactly what Griffith meant. As perfect a hiding spot as this was, it was only a matter of time until they were discovered. And she was certain Griffith had seen the ushers searching the bleachers not far from where they stood, just like she had. One inning in the same spot was long enough. Ruby needed to find their next safe lookout.

"Follow me, boys!"

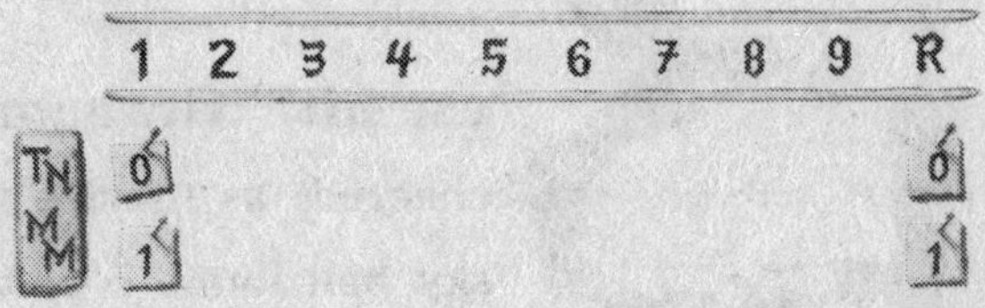

9

★

One River, Two Rivers

ase hit!" Graham cheered as Scribe's sky ball found a soft patch of turf in front of Wee Willie Nance in left garden.

"That's more like it!" Ruby cried, shaking the baseball. "I sense a rally."

The three Paynes had decided it was okay to hold their baseball here, since everyone around them had their eyes peeled to the pitch.

Griffith scanned the stands. They sat

among the cranks in the bleachers down the left garden line, almost in the very spot where the Chancellor's men had demanded their baseball a short time ago. At first Griffith hadn't grasped why Ruby would select this location, but once they sat down, he understood her logic. The last place the Chancellor's men would look would be at the scene of the attempted heist. At least for now.

Unfortunately, down on the field, any chance of a rally ended with the next whip of the willow. Doc Lindy grounded a bug bruiser right at second sack man Ed Abbatichio, who flipped the pill to Germany Smith at shortstop, who in turn fired it across the infield to Perry Werden to complete the double play.

Then Professor Lance stepped to the line. Guessing that every pitch that reached the backstop's mitt—even on a bounce—would be called a strike, he swung at and missed three straight out-of-the-strike-zone

WHIP OF THE WILLOW: *swing of the bat.*

BUG BRUISER: *ground ball. Also known as "daisy cutter" (see page 83) or "grass clipper" (see page 93).*

SECOND SACK MAN: *second baseman. The first baseman was often called "first sack man" and the third baseman was often called "third sack man."*

STEP TO THE LINE (v.): *to prepare to hit.*

BACKSTOP: *catcher.*

pitches for the final out of the top of the second frame.

"Look!" Griffith shouted.

As Preacher Wil stepped back onto the pitch for the bottom half of the inning, *two* waterways now began to emerge. The newer river started next to the Travelin' Nine dugout, flowed between shortstop and second base, and streamed all the way to the left garden wall. It separated Crazy Feet, Bubbles, and Doc Lindy from the rest of the Rough Riders.

"Do you see this?" Ruby asked.

"What kind of question is that?" replied Graham. "Of course we see this!"

"But the cranks can't," Griffith noted, motioning to fans around them who weren't reacting.

"Look at the way the rivers have split up the ballists." Ruby pointed. "It's the same way they're divided over Preacher Wil."

Two waterways now began to emerge.

Woody, Tales, and the Professor—the three who felt Preacher Wil's skin color would pose problems—were cut off from the rest of the squad on the right side of the field. Bubbles, Doc, and Crazy Feet—the three who questioned whether Preacher Wil should play because he hadn't been in Cuba—were cut off on the left. And Scribe and Guy—the two ballists who believed that Preacher Wil should play and pitch—were caught with Preacher Wil in the middle between the two rivers.

"That's what I was afraid might happen," said Ruby.

"And I'm afraid we need to leave again," Griffith added, having spotted a pair of men in suits with pink pocket squares a couple of sections over heading in their direction. "Let's go."

Ruby dropped the baseball back into her pocket and began to lead her brothers away.

Since there was open seating, except for the field-level box seats, and tickets were being checked on the plaza in front of the park, it was quite easy to move around the stadium. Once someone entered the park, they were free to go anywhere on the grounds, except on the field or in the box seats.

Hurrying through the third base line bleachers, Griffith, Ruby, and Graham ran behind the foul pole. They passed above the alcove where they had watched the first frame and scampered all the way around the outer garden, hopping back into the bleachers after turning the corner around the right garden foul pole. Then they headed up. Running the stairs two at a time, they didn't stop until they reached the third-to-last row, deep in the corner.

"These are great seats!" Graham proclaimed. "The ballists look like ants from here."

"They do look like ants, Grammy," agreed Griffith. "Maybe you should play for the Travelin' Nine. You'd fit right in."

However, Griffith was hardly in a joking frame of mind. Trying to stay one step ahead of the Chancellor's men was challenging, and it was still only the second frame. How were they going to keep this up for nine innings?

Looking around, Griffith placed a hand over his face and hid his frown. They couldn't stay in this spot for long either. They were in a corner with only one way out. If the Chancellor's men were to find them here, they would be trapped.

"Right after this half frame we're on the move," Griffith told his brother and sister, as they joined hands once more on the baseball.

"Again?" Graham asked. "Already?"

Down on the field, the second inning wasn't proceeding any better than the first for the barnstormers. Ed Abbatichio was already standing on third sack when Walter Wilmot settled in at the line. He swung at Preacher Wil's first pitch and launched a long cloud hunter to right. Woody gave chase but slowed down when he saw the river. However, instead of stopping, Woody leaped toward the water. Landing on a piece of floating lumber, he rode the river like a champion logroller and somehow made the catch. But since the ball was hit so far, the runner on third was able to tag up. The sacrifice fly plated a second Millers tally.

"Way to use the wood, Woody!" Ruby cheered.

As Wee Willie Nance headed for the plate, Graham pulled the baseball away from the others.

"I'm going to hold *my* baseball for this striker," he said. He motioned to the field with the ball, whose stitching was looser than ever.

TAG UP (*v.*): *to advance to the next base after a fly-ball out.*

SACRIFICE FLY: *fly-ball out that advances a runner.*

PLATE (*v.*): *to score a run or tally.*

TALLY: *run scored. On some fields, whenever the home team scored, a tally bell would sound. The tally keeper was the official scorer, or scorekeeper.*

He rode the river like a champion logroller.

Doc Nance took two pitches before lacing a Preacher Wil curveball into dead center. That also happened to have been where Graham was pointing and Scribe was standing. The Travelin' Nine's supersize scout snared the rawhide for the second out.

"That was easy," said Graham, breathing on the baseball and then rubbing it against his chest. "Looks like I may be the secret to the Travelin' Nine's success after all."

Ruby rolled her eyes. "If you say so," she said.

"I do say so," Graham declared. He waved the ball in Doc Lindy's direction at third sack. "Now watch this."

Up stepped Kid McNeely. After taking a pitch, he bounced a routine bug bruiser toward first sack, where Professor Lance gloved the ball cleanly and toed the bag for the third out.

"I rest my case," Graham declared.

"What case?" Ruby asked. "You were

waving the ball in the *opposite* direction."

"An out's an out!"

As Griffith, Ruby, and Graham wound through the jam-packed bleachers toward their next spot, they watched the action unfold on the field. Bubbles struck out to lead off the third frame, but Guy followed with a clean base hit up the middle. When the three Paynes finally arrived at their new vantage point on the opposite side of the stadium from where they'd been—a few rows up behind the Travelin' Nine's dugout—Preacher Wil was stepping to the plate for the first time. Like he had prior to taking the bump, he reached under his collar for his necklace, twirled the charm in his fingers, and kissed it gently.

BUMP: *pitcher's mound. Also called "hill"* *(see page 85).*

LUMBER: *baseball bat. Also called "timber"* *(see page 97).*

Digging in at the dish, Preacher Wil aimed his lumber toward left garden and stared down Kid McNeely. Then he smacked a first-pitch single to the exact spot he had pointed at.

"Way to go!" Ruby jumped up.

Griffith immediately pulled her back down so she wouldn't be spotted.

"All hands on the ball," Graham ordered with Crazy Feet stepping to the line.

Griffith surveyed the situation as the three siblings joined hands. The Travelin' Nine needed to manufacture tallies. With runners on first and second and only one out, it was the perfect time for the hit-and-run.

And the hit-and-run was on!

As soon as Kid McNeely rocked into his windup, Guy broke from second sack, and Preacher Wil took off from first. Like he had in his first at bat, Crazy Feet swung at the initial pitch. But this time, instead of tapping weakly down to first, he scorched a frozen rope Werden's way. The ball headed right for the first baseman's face! In an act of desperate self-defense, Werden raised his leather and snagged the pill inches before it took out his teeth. Then he stomped on first for the rally-killing and inning-ending double play.

HIT-AND-RUN: *a play in which a batter swings at the pitch while the base runner attempts to steal a base.*

FROZEN ROPE: *hard line drive or throw.*

LEATHER: *baseball glove or mitt.*

The Travelin' Nine's hit-and-run strategy had backfired.

"I'm putting this away," Ruby said, holding up the ball and then dropping it into her pocket.

"Why would you do that?" asked Graham.

"Because it's not helping the barnstormers," Ruby replied. "The magical things are working against them."

"I'm not sure if tucking it away is the answer," said Griffith.

As the Travelin' Nine took the field for the bottom of the inning, both raging rivers reappeared. In addition, the weather grew decidedly warmer and muggier.

However, the stickier conditions appeared to add even more movement to Preacher Wil's pitches. His offerings danced and dove en route to the dish. He easily disposed of Germany Smith on a pop-up to Tales, and he dismissed Jay Andrews on a sky ball to Doc Lindy.

"Nice work, Preacher Wil," Griffith cheered. "That's the way to clear the table setters."

But then the Millers strung together back-to-back singles, and these were no ordinary base knocks. Under normal circumstances, the routine sky balls to the outer garden would've been easy outs. However, both of these hits found the water *and* a rock, ricocheting unpredictably. The first one kicked from left garden all the way back behind home plate. The second hit pinballed from river to river before coming to rest by Preacher Wil on the hill just after the Millers had scored another run.

BASE KNOCK: *hit.*

Ruby gazed to the heavens.

Could it be that he doesn't belong? Am I wrong?

No, she told herself, as she had before the start of the match. Preacher Wil definitely belonged. She refused to allow herself to waver.

Suddenly Ruby felt the urge to *confront* the Travelin' Nine. Preacher Wil was keeping them in the contest. In fact, the Travelin' Nine's southpaw hurler had just now prevented further damage when he retired Perry Werden on a routine comebacker, fooling the Millers' striker with a beautiful breaking ball. The Rough Riders needed to be told that *they* were the reason the magic wasn't helping. Because the barnstormers were divided, they couldn't possibly win. They needed to be together. Always.

COMEBACKER: *ground ball hit directly to the pitcher.*

BREAKING BALL: *curveball.*

As she watched the Travelin' Nine head back toward the dugout, Ruby noticed something. Up until now, the ushers had been patrolling one end of every aisle. But at this moment, the closest ones she spotted had found seats a section over and were watching the game.

The time had come.

	1	2	3	4	5	6	7	8	9	R
TN	0	0	0							0
MM	1	1	1							3

10

A Dugout Divided

hat?" Griffith and Graham said together.

Ruby flipped the hair off the back of her neck. "You heard me," she said. "We're going into the dugout. Now."

Before her brothers had a chance to question her decision, Ruby was off. Paying no mind to the cranks, vendors, or ushers seated in the adjacent section, she walked down the aisle until she reached the field. Then, without so much as peeking over her shoulder, she hopped the railing and swung around the corner into the dugout.

Griffith shrugged. "I guess we're heading for the bench."

Seconds later, Griffith and Graham stood alongside Ruby inside the Travelin' Nine dugout.

Dog spotted the three Paynes first. Bounding by the ballists, he greeted Griffith with two large paws to the chest, nearly knocking him to the ground.

"Kids!" Elizabeth cried. She rushed over and group-hugged all three.

"Look who's here!" declared Tales.

"Welcome home!" Doc Lindy applauded.

"Are you okay?" asked Elizabeth, ruffling Griffith's hair. He had knelt to pet Dog.

"We're fine," Griffith replied while Dog licked his face. "I promised you we would be."

"Has anyone tried anything?" she asked. She pulled Graham closer.

"I reckon we should keep it down in here," Woody said before Graham could answer. "We don't want to call attention to these kids."

"Woody's right," Happy added. He patted the bench to his left. "Ruby, come sit. Tell me what we need to do with this water, because I don't want it coming in here. I don't know how to swim."

But Ruby didn't want to sit down. Nor did she want to keep it down. She needed to be heard, and she didn't have much time.

"The magic isn't working because of all of you," she said. She climbed onto the front dugout steps and stood before the ballists. "The magic won't work until you're together."

"The magic isn't working because someone is playing who shouldn't be," Tales countered.

"I reckon we may wish to reconsider our decision," Woody added.

"The magic isn't working because of all of you."

Ruby couldn't believe her ears. She had felt the divide in the dugout the moment she had stepped in, but the rift among the Rough Riders was even worse than she had anticipated. She glanced over her shoulder. For the time being, the umpire was chatting with some of the Millers' infielders, but shortly he would be ordering the next Travelin' Nine striker to the line. Ruby was running out of time.

She crossed her arms and looked up to Scribe. The center scout now stood next to her, and even though he wasn't on the stairs, she still barely came up to his shoulders.

"Thirty-one," she muttered.

"What'd you say that for?" asked Scribe.

Ruby didn't answer. The words seemed to come out on their own. Her thoughts returned to Chicago, when Graham had said the number. Ruby bit her lower lip. Thirty-one. Three and one. She knew exactly what it meant. There were three factions in the dugout, but they were supposed to be one team. She needed to figure out how to make the three become one.

She faced Tales and Woody again. "I thought Preacher Wil's skin color didn't matter to you."

"It doesn't," said Tales. He pointed to the cranks. "It matters to them." Then he motioned to the umpire. "And based on his calls, it apparently matters to him, too."

"It obviously does matter to you," Ruby argued. "If you're saying he's the reason the magic is working against us, then how come—"

"We need to focus on the game," the Professor interrupted. "Now is not the time for this debate."

"I reluctantly voted in favor of Preacher Wil," stated Doc Lindy, stepping forward, "and I'm glad I voted the way I did. He's more than earned my respect. He's had to endure this hot and steamy weather, this awful arbiter, and these unsportsmanlike fans. If not for his pitching, we'd be *drowning* out there."

"He's winning me over as well," Bubbles added, nodding in Preacher Wil's direction. "I'm not as convinced as Doc, but it's hard not to admire a ballist who conducts himself with such grace and honor."

Ruby scanned the barnstormers, finally resting her eyes on Preacher Wil. He sat at the far end of the bench, wearing the same warm and patient expression he always did (except for when he took the hill).

"Preacher Wil," Ruby called, "can you see the rivers on the field?"

He answered with a simple nod.

"What more proof do you need?" Ruby asked, her pleading eyes returning to Tales and the Professor. "Doesn't that tell you he belongs?"

"I reckon he can see the rivers because he's out there with the Travelin' Nine,"

Woody answered. "But that don't necess'rily mean he belongs with us."

"You've trusted us all along," continued Ruby, the desperation in her voice building. "We need you to trust us now. We need you to come together as a team because—"

"Excuse me," a voice said, "you're not permitted in here."

Everyone turned. Three ushers appeared at the end of the dugout. One was motioning to Griffith, Ruby, and Graham.

"The rules are very clear," said a second usher. "You need to come with us."

Dog stepped in front of Griffith and growled.

"It's okay, boy," Griffith said, patting Dog's belly.

"Take Dog with you," Preacher Wil suggested. "I don't think he likes being down here."

"Thanks, Preacher Wil," Griffith replied. "But we—"

Dog stepped in front of Griffith.

"I insist." He cut Griffith off. "Take Dog."

"The game is about to resume," the third usher said. "Let's go. Now!"

Griffith gazed over at Happy and Scribe. Neither ballist appeared to be suspicious of these particular ushers. But then Griffith faced his mother, and there was no denying her terror. She also sensed that these men couldn't tell the difference between a ticket stub and a hot dog. They were the Chancellor's goons.

"Okay, we'll take Dog," Griffith said, hoping to ease his mother's fears.

What if something happens to Dog?

Blinking hard, Griffith erased the thought from his head. He couldn't allow himself to think that.

"We'll be fine," Griffith assured the barnstormers, as he gathered his brother and sister. "Try not to worry about us. We'll see you after the game."

At the end of the dugout, one of the ushers held open the gate as Griffith, Ruby, Graham, and Dog all filed through. They followed the other two ushers up the aisle.

"I'm right behind you," the third usher said, trying to close the dugout door. He kicked over the bucket of balls that had been propping it open.

Griffith peeked back. The trailing usher was temporarily distracted. This was their chance.

"Run!" Griffith whispered. "That way!"

Before the two ushers in front could turn around, he began leading his brother, sister, and Dog through the bleachers. Dodging the cranks, ducking under railings, and running on the benches, they fled down the left garden line. But because the ushers were large adults, they couldn't fit under the bars. Nor could they maneuver through the crowd as easily, and they were forced to run all the way up the aisle to the break in the railing. Which was where they encountered a vendor in the middle of a sale who refused to budge.

"You can't run forever!" one usher shouted.

Using their size to their advantage, Griffith, Ruby, Graham, and Dog had managed to escape . . . for now.

	1	2	3	4	5	6	7	8	9	R
TN	0	0	0							0
MM	1	1	1							3

11

★

Twists and Spouts

ollow me!” Ruby ordered. With her brothers and Dog tailing close behind, Ruby charged up the narrow aisle. They darted down a runway that led out of the bleachers, ran halfway around the promenade, and reentered the grandstands behind home plate.

“We’re going up there!” Ruby pointed into the crowd.

“But—”

“Not now!” Ruby cut Graham off. “We need to make sure we’ve lost them.”

Racing up the steps, they climbed all the way to the top of the bleachers until they reached a door.

"Are we going in there?" asked Graham.

After a quick glance at Griffith, Ruby pulled open the door. High above the field and directly behind home plate, she had found a storage closet. It was filled with lumber, the same type used to construct the bleachers. They shuffled in, and Ruby shut the door.

"Help me stack these up," Griffith said to Graham.

Close to the ceiling of the closet were small, rectangular windows. So Griffith and Graham piled up some of the planks, and in moments they were watching the action.

On the field, the Travelin' Nine were down to their last out in the fourth. At the plate stood Scribe (who looked enormous even from this far away), but he already had two strikes against him.

In moments they were watching the action.

"C'mon, Scribe!" Ruby cheered, and as if the center scout had heard her call, he lashed a base hit to right garden.

Up stepped Doc. Kid McNeely's first pitch was high, and even this umpire had to call it a ball because the pill soared three feet over the catcher's mitt. Doc swatted the next offering into left garden. Wee Willie Nance charged hard, but the ball dropped in just beneath his leather.

"Out!" the umpire called, even though the rock had clearly landed safely. "Three hands dead!"

As much as he may have wanted to, Doc didn't dare contest the call. The other Rough Riders resisted the urge to argue as well. To a man, the ballists realized they could little afford to have a single player ejected from the game. All they could do was accept the unfair ruling and take the field for the bottom of the frame.

While the barnstormers reemerged from the dugout, Griffith searched the crowd. It worried him that he and his siblings were in a small space with only a single exit. If any of the Chancellor's men detected them, they would be cornered. But at the moment, Griffith didn't see any of the thugs around, and he felt they were hidden enough to stay here another half frame.

Of course, the rivers returned as soon as the ballists took the pitch. However, the waterways reappeared with a *twist*. A water-spout began to form slowly on the river to the right, and with each warm-up toss that Preacher Wil threw, another one emerged. By the time he was ready to throw his first pitch, a half dozen of them were dancing on the water.

With the windstorms brewing in right, Ruby reflexively reached for her pocket. But she stopped herself. The magic wasn't going to help the barnstormers until they were united behind Preacher Wil.

The Travelin' Nine hurler received the signs from Guy and then shifted his stare to Ed Abbatichio, the Millers' first striker. Even as he threw the pitch, Preacher Wil's eyes didn't leave the batter. Unnerved by a hurler who wasn't looking at his target, Abbatichio stepped from the line as he swung. He grounded meekly to Professor Lance, who fielded the easy daisy cutter and stepped on the sack for the first out.

Walter Wilmot fared no better. The Millers' player-manager was equally disarmed by Preacher Wil's stare tactic. He lined the first pitch right at Doc Lindy down at third for the second out of the frame.

"One more, Preacher Wil!" Graham cheered.

Ruby held her breath. So far, the water-spouts hadn't had any effect on the action.

Preacher Wil's strong pitching had stymied the first two strikers. All he needed to do was retire Wee Willie Nance, one of the weakest hitters in the home team's lineup. She glanced at Griffith, who pumped an encouraging fist in her direction.

"You can do it," Ruby whispered through gritted teeth. "C'mon, Preacher Wil."

At the dish, Wee Willie Nance's timber trembled as Preacher Wil glared in. Wanting off the striker's line as fast as possible, he also swung at the first pitch, looping a soft liner toward Tales at second. Tales lifted his leather and . . .

STRIKER'S LINE: *batter's box.*

Whoosh!

The easy pop-up was sucked into a waterspout! Higher and higher it rose. Faster and faster it spun. Of course, all the locals could see was a flying pill that seemed to have a mind of its own.

Suddenly the baseball shot from the spout

and disappeared in the distance over the right garden fence.

Home run!

The Millers had plated yet another run. They now led 4 to 0.

Even as Preacher Wil was recording the last out of the frame, Ruby's hopes were fading. For a few moments, she had allowed herself to believe that Preacher Wil could overcome the strange events working against the Travelin' Nine on the field. But that was next to impossible with a team in turmoil.

"Look," Graham said, pointing to the far corner of the storage closet. "Another door."

With Dog by his side, Griffith walked over and removed the slats of wood that had mostly hidden the door. "What do you think?" he asked, glancing back to his sister.

Ruby hadn't considered moving from where they were. They had finally found a spot where the ushers wouldn't see them. Still, as long as they stayed out of plain sight, she saw no harm in checking where the door led.

"Let's give it a shot," she said. She peeked down at the field. "It's still between innings. We can always come back here to watch the fifth."

Walking past her brothers and Dog, Ruby opened the door for Griffith, and he headed in. He led them through a barely lit and narrow passageway that sloped upward and ran along the back of the stadium. The ceiling gradually became lower, and even Graham had to duck.

"I think we're in the rafters," Ruby stated.

"We must be," agreed Griffith. "We're behind the bleacher walls. These are the catwalks."

"Wherever we are," Graham said, bringing up the rear, "it sure is dark."

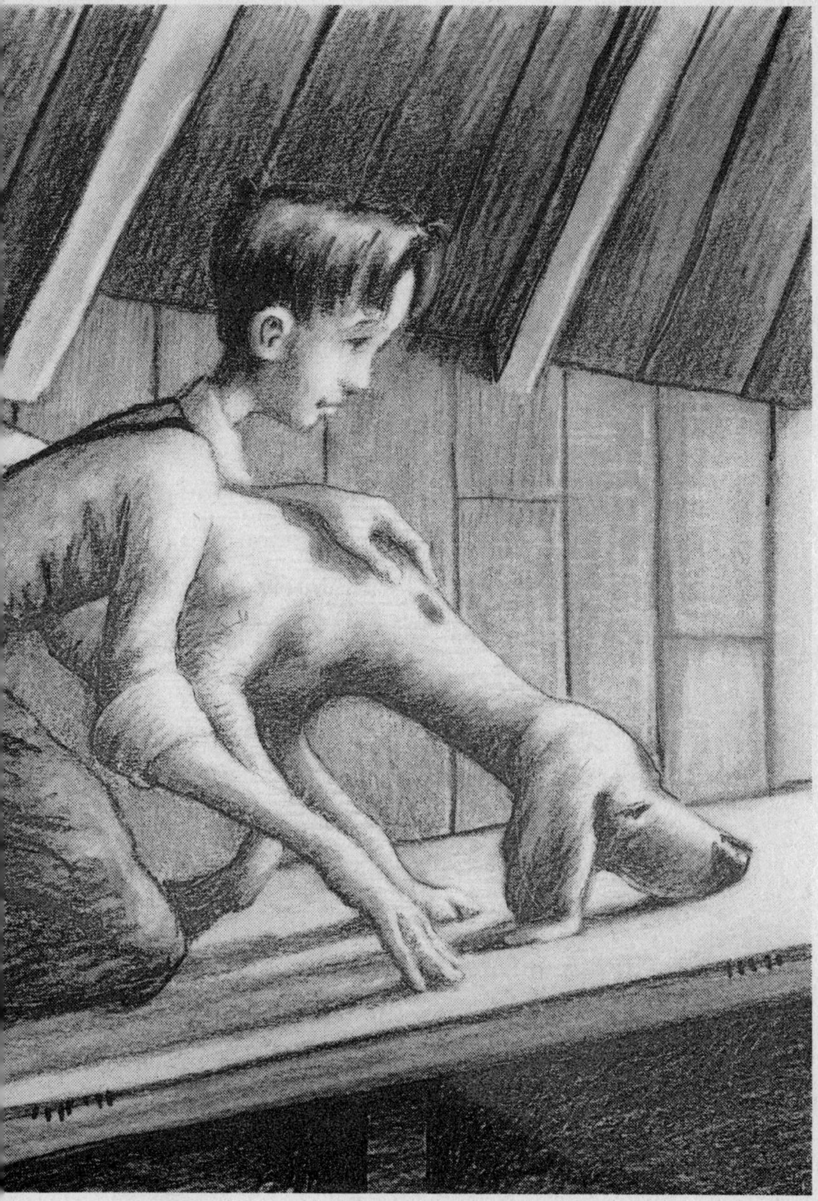

"I think we're in the rafters."

"Wow, Grammy," Ruby said with a snicker. "You figured that out all by yourself? Good work."

Clunk!

Ruby smacked her head on a beam.

"Ow!" she cried.

"That's what you get for teasing me." Graham chuckled. "And that's what you get for keeping secrets from me and for—"

"Everyone, stop!" Griffith interrupted. He held out both arms. "We've reached the end of the catwalk."

All three Paynes and Dog peered over the edge of the passageway.

"There's a ladder." Graham knelt down and pointed. "And I see someone down there!"

Griffith squatted down next to his brother, and as soon as he saw the bald-headed man seated on the stool with the scorecard in his lap, he knew exactly where they were.

"We're in the scoreboard," Griffith whispered. "The one way up high behind home dish."

Ruby leaned over her brothers for a closer look. "We sure are." She motioned to the rope hanging from the beam beside the man. "There's the cord for the tally bell."

"And there's the tally bell!" Graham declared, pointing farther up the wall. "That means we're at the top of Nicollet Park!" He jumped to his feet and patted the low ceiling. "Now this is what I call a bird's-eye view. We have to watch this frame from up here. Please."

Ruby stood up and stepped to the wall on her right. Through one of the few knotholes at eye level, she gazed down at the field. The view wasn't nearly as clear as it had been from the storage room windows, but she still could see all the action. Inching away from the knothole, she peered over at the tally keeper again. So long as they stood back from the edge and didn't make much noise, they would be fine.

Unfortunately, the Travelin' Nine were anything but fine. The Professor struck out on three wild pitches he *had* to swing at. Then Bubbles looked like he had beaten out an infield hit, but the umpire called him out.

Griffith rubbed his temples with his fingers. "Why doesn't that umpire put on a Millers uniform?" he muttered, echoing Graham's sentiment from the first frame.

However, Guy lashed a clean base hit up the middle. And then Preacher Wil—after twirling his necklace in his fingers and kissing it gently—slapped a single to right garden. All of a sudden, the Travelin' Nine had two runners on with Crazy Feet stepping to the dish. With one swing of the timber, he could cut the lead to a single run.

"Put us on the scoreboard," Ruby pleaded under her breath.

Kid McNeely's first pitch was right over the heart of the plate, but Crazy Feet didn't swing. He took the second pitch as well, another perfect strike.

"Why didn't he swing?" Griffith held his head. "What's he doing up there?"

With a count of no balls and two strikes, Crazy Feet needed to protect the plate. Leaning out over the dish, he prepared for the pitch. The Millers' hurler reared back and fired—an inside heater heading right at Crazy Feet. The barnstormers' left scout whirled to avoid the rock, but he couldn't get out of the way. The ball hit the spinning Crazy Feet squarely between the shoulder blades.

"Strike three!" the umpire bellowed. "Yer out! Three hands dead!"

A stunned Crazy Feet dropped his lumber. The Rough Riders in the dugout rose to the top step. The three Paynes in the scoreboard gasped.

"When you turned to avoid the pitch," the umpire shouted, pointing at Crazy Feet, "you swung. You will not be awarded first base. Strike three! Yer out!"

Ruby stepped away from the wall and held her closed journal over her face. She wanted to cry. So long as the Travelin' Nine weren't united behind Preacher Wil, there was nothing she and her brothers could do. It didn't matter if they did or didn't hold their baseball. Nor did it matter if they were focused solely on the game and thinking only positive thoughts.

Still, Ruby couldn't allow herself to lose faith. The barnstormers *could* come back against the Millers. Despite the umpire and the obstacles, Preacher Wil was tossing a gem, and Scribe, Guy, and Preacher Wil were all hitting Kid McNeely's best pitches.

Yes, there were glimmers of hope, but the Travelin' Nine were beginning to run out of baseball.

She walked back to the wall, and for a brief moment, she allowed her frustration to boil over. Ruby pounded the wood with her fist. A shower of splinters flew out, and the round knothole that Ruby had used before suddenly resembled a teardrop.

Griffith gasped. He raced to the edge of the passageway and peered down. Luckily, the tally keeper hadn't heard Ruby's punch over the roar of the crowd. And the tiny pieces of wood had all landed harmlessly on the floor of the catwalk.

"That was close," Griffith said, stepping over to his sister and brother.

"Dog thought so too." Graham pointed to Dog, who was growling.

"We have to figure this out!" said Ruby, her voice shaking.

"We will." Griffith placed his hand on Ruby's shoulder.

"But we're running out of time." She lifted the baseball from her pocket for the first time in two innings.

"You'll figure it out," Graham said, draping his arm around Ruby. "I'm sure you will."

"I know we're missing something," she said. "I know Preacher Wil belongs with us. I know . . ."

Ruby stopped herself because if she said another word, she would start to cry. She looked down at the disintegrating ball in her hand and inserted her pinky into the acorn-size hole. Then her brothers both placed their hands atop the baseball.

And at that moment, Ruby was no longer able to fend off her tears. A single drop fell from the corner of her eye and landed on the baseball.

The three Paynes felt the ball *shiver*.

Clunk. Clunk.

Suddenly Dog growled louder. His floppy ears perked up as he inched closer to Ruby's knothole. Staring into the sky, Dog arched his back and flexed his hind legs, as if he was preparing to leap out (if he could fit).

"What is it, Dog?" Griffith asked. "What's the matter?"

All three stepped toward the knothole.

"Ahhhh!"

Griffith, Ruby, and Graham screamed as one.

Dog yelped.

All four jumped away.

An enormous eye stared back at them through the tear-shaped hole. The eye, which was surrounded by feathers, looked at each of the three kids and then *soared* off.

The Paynes raced to their knotholes in time to see the bird flying over right garden.

"Now that's what I *really* call a bird's-eye view!" Graham said.

"That's our bald eagle!" exclaimed Ruby.

"Without a doubt!" Griffith added. "Don't lose sight of it."

High above the field the eagle soared. It swooped down over the infield and then rose back toward the heavens over the right garden bleachers. It circled the scoreboard a few times and then settled on top of the flagpole in the outer garden.

"That's why he was growling," said Griffith, patting the hound's belly. He glanced down at Dog, and for a second, he thought Dog had *winked* at him.

Perched on the flagpole across the field, the eagle raised a single wing and flapped it once. Then the bird raised the other wing and made the same motion.

"What's it doing?" Graham asked.

"It's looking right at us," said Griffith.

"He's waving." Ruby nodded. "He's waving to us." She looked to her brothers. "The eagle's telling us to come with him."

"Look!" Graham pointed.

The bald eagle was airborne again. It flew straight across the field and disappeared behind them in the direction of the entranceway to the stadium.

"Come on!" shouted Ruby.

They raced back along the dark corridor and through the storage closet. Then they charged down the bleachers, rounded the corner onto a ramp that led out of the stands, and headed for the front of Nicollet Park.

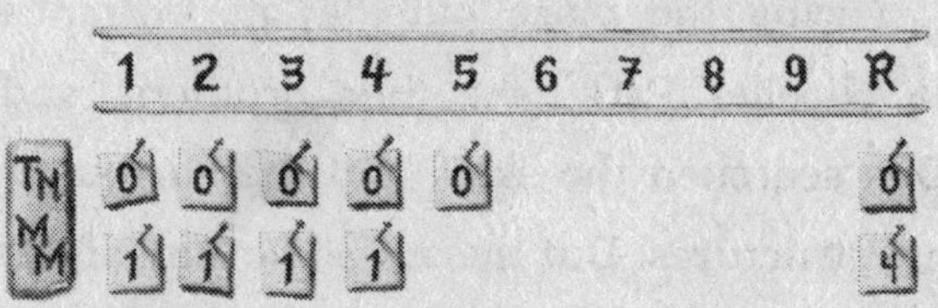

12

★

The Man from the Trolley, the Man from the Park

here did it go?” Graham asked.

“Just keep looking,” urged Ruby.

Facing the plaza outside the entrance to Nicollet Park, she, her brothers, and Dog searched the skies and the surrounding structures. But there was no sign of the eagle.

One minute passed. Two minutes. Five.

“How long are we going to stand here?”

Graham asked, folding his arms across his chest.

Ruby glared at him sideways. "As long as it takes, Grammy," she snapped.

Griffith shook his head once at Ruby and then rested his hand on Graham's shoulder. "We need to be patient," he said.

"*She* needs to be patient," Graham said, peeking around Griffith to make a face at his sister.

Ruby chewed the inside of her cheek. *How long do we wait?* The eagle had to have been a sign. Even her brothers were convinced it was. So where did it go? What were they still missing?

She glanced over her shoulder. The lone usher sitting on a wooden stool just inside the front gate hadn't yet noticed them. Along with everyone else, he was watching the game, since all the cranks were already inside. In fact, the man had his back to the three Paynes. When the time came to reenter, they wouldn't have any problem sneaking past him and . . .

Dog began to *purr*. He stepped forward and stared across the plaza.

"Do you see someone, boy?" Ruby asked.

Kneeling down to Dog's level, she saw what he did. Across Blaisdell Avenue, a man stood against a red brick building. She squinted and leaned in for a better look, but because of the shadow cast by an awning, all she could see was the man's long, grayish beard. She glanced up at Griffith. His face had turned ghostly white.

"Griff, what's the matter?" said Ruby.

Griffith opened his mouth, but the words didn't form.

Ruby stood. "What is it?" she asked, her voice trembling. "Tell me." She spun to Graham. He too wore a stunned expression. "Grammy, what's wrong?"

All she could see was the man's long, grayish beard.

But all Graham could do was point.

Ruby peered across the way again. The man had stepped from the building and was now in plain view. His clothing was worn and tattered.

"Will one of you say something?" Ruby pleaded, her eyes shifting from brother to brother.

"That's the man . . ." Griffith finally began to speak. He swallowed. "That's the man I saw in Jackson Park. Back in Chicago."

"That's . . ." Graham started and stopped. "That's the man . . ." He stopped again.

"What, Grammy?" Ruby placed her hand behind Graham's neck. "Tell me," she urged.

Graham let out several short breaths. "That's the man . . . That's the man I saw. On the trolley."

"What man?" asked Griffith, turning to his brother.

"What trolley?" Ruby asked.

"In Louisville," Graham answered. "On the way to Churchill Downs."

"You never told us you saw anyone." Ruby leaned in closer.

Graham shook his head.

"Why didn't you?" Ruby asked.

Graham shrugged.

"You're absolutely sure it's him?" said Griffith, stepping around Dog so he could look his brother in the eye.

"Of course," Graham replied, gesturing across the plaza. "How often do you see someone who looks like *that*?"

All three looked out at the man. He wore no shoes, his clothes were filthy, and a long, unkempt beard hung down, reaching a point just above his belt.

Griffith nodded. "I'm sure it was the same man I saw. It's also why—"

Dog's growl interrupted Griffith, the same

growl he had made in the scoreboard a short time ago. And like before, Dog's ears perked up as high as they could go.

Suddenly the bald eagle reappeared. It emerged from behind and swooped down. It dove in so close to the three Paynes that the tip of a wing clipped the top of Griffith's head and the breeze from its pumping wings blew all of their hair. Then the eagle soared across the plaza to circle over the old man's head. The man raised his arm, and the great bird darted in his direction, landing on his already torn sleeve, tears in the shape of talons.

"They're together," Griffith noted. "The eagle and the old man are with each other."

The man peered across the plaza. By now there was no doubt he was looking at the three of them just as intently as they were looking at him. He held their gaze as the eagle lifted a talon and tapped the man's fingers.

"What are they trying to tell us?" Ruby asked.

But before Griffith could respond, the old man turned and disappeared around the corner onto West 31st Street.

"Come on!" shouted Griffith, waving to the others.

All three and Dog tore through the plaza and bolted across Blaisdell Avenue. Turning the corner, they nearly charged right into the old man, who stood with his back against the brick building. The majestic bird sat tall on the man's raised, bent arm.

"You've been following us," Ruby said. "What do you want?"

"I am here to help you." The man's different-colored eyes danced from Payne to Payne to Payne.

"I saw you in Louisville," said Graham.

"I saw you the other day in Chicago," Griffith added. Then he pointed to the eagle. "And I first saw you on the steamer to Louisville."

"Why are you following us?" Ruby asked.

"I am here to help you," the old man repeated. He peeked his head around the corner, glanced back toward the stadium, and then looked again at the three kids. "I can provide you with assistance and answers. Much assistance and many answers. But they mustn't learn I'm here."

"Who's they?"

"I think you know the answer to that, Mr. Griffith."

Griffith's eyes bulged. "How do you know who I am?"

The old man pinched his wire-rimmed glasses and smiled. "You're Mr. Griffith, she's Miss Ruby, he's Mr. Graham, and this one here's name is Dog." He reached down and scratched behind the hound's ears. "Yes, I know all of you."

The old man spoke in a polished manner, with perfect grammar and diction, and with a confidence that seemed inconsistent with his appearance. He sounded nothing like Griffith had imagined.

"How do you know who we are?" Graham asked.

"How do we know we can trust you?" added Ruby, eyeing him sideways.

Griffith studied the old man, staring into the deep creases and winding wrinkles that crisscrossed his face.

"We can trust him," Griffith said, turning to his sister and brother. "If he wanted to do harm to us, he would've long ago. And look at Dog." Griffith reached down and placed his hand under the hound's chin. "There's no better judge of character. If this man was a danger, Dog would've told us."

"You are correct, Mr. Griffith," said the old man, his different-colored eyes blinking as he spoke. "I will not harm you. I will do everything in my power to help you." He peeked nervously around the corner again and then looked back at the three Paynes. "Today I am here to warn you."

"Warn us about what?" Ruby asked. She

felt the hairs on her arms begin to tingle.

"There is no time for me to provide you with all the details, but trust me when I tell you, there is one amongst you who cannot be trusted."

"What does that mean?" Graham asked.

"I don't understand," Ruby added.

Griffith glanced up at the eagle. The majestic bird, who was even closer to Griffith than he'd been back on the *Meriwether*, was nodding.

The old man pinched his glasses again. "One who is with you is not with you at all."

"One of the Travelin' Nine?" Ruby pressed.

"Yes, but I don't yet know who."

Suddenly the eagle spread its enormous wings and raised them to the skies. Griffith, Ruby, and Graham jumped backward, but the old man didn't even flinch. He merely turned his head to the bird still perched on his sleeve and nodded.

"We must go now," the old man said. He looked to Griffith. "I'm quite confident we will be seeing one another before you depart the Mill City."

As the old man spoke, Ruby's gaze remained fixed on the eagle. Once again, the bird lifted a talon and tapped the old man's fingers. What was the eagle trying to tell her?

"Watch out for them," the old man said, pointing back toward the plaza. "They are evil and cruel."

Griffith, Ruby, Graham, and Dog stepped toward the corner and looked across the plaza at Nicollet Park. Then they turned back to the old man and the eagle.

But they were already gone. Disappeared. As if they had never been there.

Except for the feather that Graham picked up.

"I was right!" he exclaimed, jubilant. He

waved the enormous plume at his brother and sister.

"Right about what?" asked Ruby, eyeing her brother sideways.

Graham grabbed a lamppost and spun around. "My birthday wish."

"Grammy, what on earth are you talking about?" Griffith stepped up to his brother.

"That old man knows about things. Things we don't. And he's going to make my birthday wish come true!"

"What birthday wish?" Ruby asked.

Graham stopped spinning and looked from Ruby to Griffith to Dog. He knew he wasn't supposed to say a wish out loud, but this wish was different. He *had* to share it.

"The old man and the eagle are going to bring Dad back."

"What?" Griffith and Ruby asked together.

"They are," Graham insisted. "Did you see the way he looked at us with those eyes?

And what about the way *our* eagle landed on his arm? That old man's a wizard or a magician, and that eagle—"

"Grams." Griffith cut him off. He placed a firm hand on his brother's shoulder. "That's not going to happen. Dad's gone forever. I know you don't want to believe that—"

"You're wrong," Graham interrupted. He slid out from under Griffith's hand. "Just you watch!"

Griffith inhaled a long breath and let it out slowly. His seven-year-old brother didn't understand that their father was never coming back. Graham still hadn't grasped what it meant to be dead, and Griffith wondered if their mother knew this. If she didn't, he had to tell her right away.

Turning back to Ruby, Griffith expected her to look equally concerned. However, Ruby was smiling, and her blue eyes sparkled.

"What is it?" Griffith asked.

Ruby waved her brothers in closer and held out the baseball she had just lifted from her pocket. The stitching appeared slightly less frayed, the seams looked a little tighter, and resting atop the ball was a tiny white feather.

"I'm not sure what that eagle was trying to tell us," Ruby said, "but I'm more certain than ever that the Rough Riders hold the key."

"But they're in the dugout," Graham said.

"We're going back there. We need to tell them everything we saw, everything that just happened."

"Even about our baseball?" asked Graham.

Ruby paused. "No, not about the baseball. Not yet. But everything else that's—"

"But what about the ushers?" Graham pressed. "How will we get past them?"

"He's going to help us with them." Ruby reached over and tapped Dog on the head with their baseball.

"They've been watching us the whole time we've been out here," said Griffith.

"The ushers?" Ruby flinched. "They have?"

Griffith nodded. "I just figured out what the old man was pointing at." He motioned to the stadium. "Look!"

All three gazed back at Nicollet Park, at the area high above home plate. Even from across the street and plaza, they were able to locate the storage closet's narrow, rectangular windows. And through those windows, Griffith, Ruby, and Graham could see the ushers looking in their direction.

"They saw everything!" Graham exclaimed. "The three of us, the old man, and the eagle, too."

"But who were they watching?" asked

Ruby, turning to Griffith. "Us or them?"

Griffith swallowed. "Us *and* them."

"We need to get back to the dugout," Ruby said. "Now!"

13

★

Back to the Dugout

gnoring the ushers, vendors, and cranks, Griffith, Ruby, Graham, and Dog dashed into the stadium and darted down the aisle to the visitors' bench. They leaped over the railing and slid into the dugout just as the Millers were leaving the field after the top half of the frame.

"Look who's back!" Bubbles announced.

"Thank goodness!" cried Elizabeth, bounding past the barnstormers. "I was so worried." She hugged each child.

"We're okay, Mom," Griffith assured her. "I told you we would be."

"Griff's taking good care of us," Ruby added.

"He is?" Graham raised his hands. "You could've fooled me! First he made us run—"

"There's no time, Grammy." Ruby cut him off by covering his mouth. "We have too much to talk about, and the barnstormers need to take the field for the sixth."

"Sixth?" Doc pointed to the center garden scoreboard. "Try eighth."

Ruby gasped. Not only had they missed the sixth inning pursuing the eagle and talking to the old man, but they had also missed the entire seventh frame and half of the eighth.

"We have some news," she announced, leaping to the top step. "We need everyone to hear it."

"I reckon we need to get back out there,"

said Woody, thumbing to the field.

"Hold on," Professor Lance said, adjusting his eye patch. "Let me see if I can buy us a couple minutes. I'll go tell the umpire we're contemplating a pitching change." He looked to Preacher Wil, standing with Dog against his leg at the end of the dugout. "We're not, but I need to give a reason for the delay. I'll be back in a moment."

As Ruby waited for the Professor, she searched the grandstands. She instantly spotted the two men dressed as ushers by an alcove next to the box seats in back of home plate. Before they had the chance to notice her, Ruby jumped off the front steps and ducked behind Scribe and Woody. She pulled her brothers with her.

"What is it?" asked Griffith.

"Just playing it safe," Ruby replied.

She felt the baseball in her pocket and thought about what the old man had just told them. If he was right—and she believed he was—one of the Travelin' Nine couldn't be trusted. There was a mole among the barnstormers. As the Professor returned to the dugout and the ballists gathered around, Ruby wondered if she really should be telling *all* of them what had just taken place.

But she decided to anyway. Somehow Ruby must convince them that they needed to come together as a team. Talking with them—with all of them—seemed to be the only option.

"We met a man," Ruby began. "A very odd-looking man."

"Odd?" asked Woody.

"He was old and had strange eyes." Ruby let out a breath. "He's following us."

"Following?" asked Tales, twitching his bushy mustache.

"But we know he's good," Griffith noted. "He's here to help us."

"Help?" Doc said.

"How do you know?" Bubbles asked.

"Let them speak," said Professor Lance, holding up his hands.

Ruby let out another breath and glanced around Bubbles at the pitch. The umpire was roaring with laughter as he chatted up Walter Wilmot and a few of the other Miller ballists. But what caught her attention were the pools of water starting to form all over the green oasis. On the infield, two large ones took shape—one in the grassy area between the pitcher's hill and third sack, one in the dirt area near second base. In the outer garden, *thousands* of tiny puddles were now dotting the playing surface, turning the field into a land of ten thousand lakes.

The Millers couldn't see any of this. As pond after pond after pond popped up all around, the hometown ballists continued to talk with the umpire. Two of the Millers were even standing in the middle of pools. And since the cranks weren't reacting to any of this, it was clear they couldn't see the waters either.

But the barnstormers could. They were all momentarily as distracted as Ruby.

"Back in Louisville," Ruby continued, turning to the ballists again, "Graham saw the old man on the trolley ride to Churchill Downs. Then Griffith saw him in Jackson Park in Chicago. And he has this bald eagle with him, the one we all saw before the fires started in Chicago."

"How do you know it's the same eagle?" Bubbles inquired.

"Tell them, Griff," she said to her older brother.

Griffith placed a hand over his stomach. "I had seen the eagle before." He paused. "I saw it on the *Meriwether*, the steamer we took to Louisville."

"Most intriguing," Happy said, resting his right hand on his chin. "Most—"

"That's it!" Ruby suddenly shouted. She pointed at Happy. "Don't move! There's the proof!"

	1	2	3	4	5	6	7	8	9	R
TN	0	0	0	0	0	0	0	0		0
MM	1	1	1	1	1	1	1			7

14

★

Hand-to-Hand

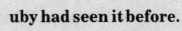

Ruby had seen it before. Dozens of times. But she had never *noticed* the coincidence until now.

"Yes!" Ruby exclaimed, charging over to Preacher Wil. She grabbed him by the arm and led him across the dugout until he stood face-to-face with Happy.

"Hold up your hand," she instructed Happy, motioning to the hand he still held to his chin.

Happy obliged.

Ruby then looked to Preacher Wil, but he needed no directions. He was already extending his left hand and turning his palm outward.

"Well, I'll be," said Bubbles, scratching what remained of his ear.

"I reckon that there is the darnedest thing I ever did see," Woody added.

The two hurlers stood hand-to-hand. Happy and Preacher Wil were missing the identical finger on their pitching hands.

"Preacher Wil belongs with the Travelin' Nine," Ruby declared.

"I'll say he does," Griffith said.

"I couldn't put my finger on why I was absolutely certain." Ruby beamed. She dropped her hand into her pocket and held their baseball. "Now I can. This is the sign I was looking for."

"I'll say it is," Doc Lindy agreed. "What are the chances of that?"

The two hurlers stood hand-to-hand.

"A billion to one!" Professor Lance answered. "Maybe more." He walked up to Preacher Wil. "My good man, I was wrong. You are a part of this team."

"Without a doubt," said Tales, shaking Preacher Wil's other hand. "I voted against your playing with us, but I was wrong. You are the replacement we need."

Woody stepped behind Ruby and placed both hands on her shoulders. "I reckon this young lady put us all through a nightmare a few days ago, but she trusted her heart. Ruby, I believe I speak for everyone when I say, please forgive us for doubting your—"

"What's going on in there?" the umpire shouted toward the Travelin' Nine dugout. "Take the field this instant. Do not delay *my* game."

Griffith peered down at the row of ballists. Each and every one wanted to give the umpire a piece of their mind (so did Griffith, for that matter), but that wasn't how the barnstormers approached the game of baseball. They let their performance on the pitch do the talking. So they bit their tongues and obeyed the order.

As the Rough Riders returned to the green oasis, the raging rivers that had divided the pitch were gone. The Travelin' Nine were back together, a single force on a field of crystal clear lakes.

"Show 'em what you're made of!" Graham cheered.

"They're about to," said Griffith, ruffling his brother's hair. "That umpire, the Millers, and every single crank in Nicollet Park are about to learn that the barnstormers never give up."

"I like the way that sounds," Ruby said, smiling as wide as the Mississippi. Then she added, "That umpire didn't see us in here."

"No, he didn't," Griffith agreed. He rested

his hand on Graham's shoulder. "I like this view. Don't you, Grams?"

"Oh yeah!" Graham cheered.

"We're not running from anyone anymore." Griffith nodded to Ruby. "We're staying right here."

	1	2	3	4	5	6	7	8	9	R
TN	0	0	0	0	0	0	0	0		0
MM	1	1	1	1	1	1	1			7

15

★

Snow Way!

Preacher Wil headed toward the hill for the last half of the eighth inning, and the Travelin' Nine applauded their hurler and teammate. Griffith, Ruby, and Graham clapped too, as they stood against the back of the dugout so as not to be detected.

Once on the mound, Preacher Wil untucked his necklace and twirled the charm in his extra-long fingers. It glistened in the sunshine. Yes, for the first time all week, rays of light began to filter through clouds; the muggy day quickly turned hot and steamy.

Graham pointed skyward. "The sun's coming through like it did at the end of the match in Chicago."

"Now it's our turn to come through," Ruby said.

Sliding between her brothers, she glanced at Happy and Dog seated at the far end of the dugout. Ruby realized it was strange—even rude—for them to be standing so far from the old-timer, but they *couldn't* be next to him.

Ruby pulled the baseball out of her pocket and smiled. The seams were tight once again, and the stitching was no longer badly frayed. The ball was back to its old, weathered self.

"Let's see what we can do to help Preacher Wil," Ruby told her brothers.

"I like the way that sounds," said Happy, walking over.

Instinctively, Ruby hid the baseball behind

her back, while her brothers jumped between her and the Rough Rider.

Happy smiled knowingly. "I'll pretend I don't know what you have there," he said, "but rest assured that I do."

"What do we have?" Graham asked too innocently. He showed his hands to Happy. "We don't have anything."

"Of course you don't." Happy faked a cough and patted his chest with his fist. "Do what you need to do. But one of these days, we should talk about what you *don't* have."

Griffith nodded to Happy. The Travelin' Nine's eldest member was right. It was time they talked about the baseball.

On the night of their father's funeral, Uncle Owen had told Griffith, Ruby, and Graham to keep the baseball a secret. Then, in his letter, he had warned them that the Chancellor mustn't find out about the ball. But the Chancellor had found out about it, and he also knew they had it. So why did the three Paynes still need to keep it a secret from the barnstormers?

Griffith would talk to Happy about their baseball. But he needed time and privacy. There would be plenty of both on the train ride to St. Louis; he would have the conversation then.

With Happy back in his seat at the opposite end of the bench, Griffith scanned the stands. Since the barnstormers were back together again, he felt as upbeat as his brother and sister. However, at the same time, he realized it wasn't going to take the ushers or the Chancellor's men an entire inning to find them. Even with their backs against the dugout wall, he, Ruby, and Graham were still in plain sight. Griffith may have told his sister and brother they were staying right here, but he knew they wouldn't be able to.

Griffith placed his hand on the ball, and then Graham added his.

"We're down seven runs," Ruby said, looking from brother to brother. She inserted her pinky into the baseball's hole. "It's going to take a Christmas miracle for the Travelin' Nine to win this match and—"

It started with a single one—no larger, smaller, or different from any they had ever seen. But since this snowflake fell from a now crystal clear sky on a suddenly blistering summer's day, everyone noticed it (well, at least all the barnstormers did). It drifted softly on a gentle breeze until it came to rest on the rawhide in Preacher Wil's hand.

The Travelin' Nine looked skyward, and the moment they did, the blue skies burst.

"A sun snowstorm!" Graham exclaimed, letting go of the baseball and raising his hands high overhead.

Ruby's bright eyes gleamed. "Our Christmas miracle!"

"A sun snowstorm!"

Fast and furious fell the snow, transforming the field into a serene sea of white. While Preacher Wil was taking his warm-up tosses, the jubilant Travelin' Nine couldn't resist frolicking. Woody juggled snowballs out in right garden, and on the left side of the diamond, Bubbles and Doc Lindy played catch with a mound the size of a cannonball. Even Dog joined in. Running out onto the *white* oasis, he bounded back and forth from base to base like a runner caught in a rundown.

Graham joined in on the fun too. Using mitts as mittens to protect his hands from the cold, he built a miniature snowman on the dugout steps.

For a few brief moments, the cold, refreshing snow on a hot August afternoon gave Griffith, Ruby, Graham, and the barnstormers a chance to celebrate. This bit of white magic brought them hope. The weight of family tragedies, financial debts, and even the Chancellor lightened enough so that they could truly play, and possibly even win. Once again they were a team. Once again they were a family.

As with all the other water events that had taken place that day, the Minneapolitans weren't able to see the snow, either. They saw only grown men (and a dog) prancing about. Needless to say, they didn't take too kindly to the sight. Some of the cranks began to boo and hiss, and some of the Millers began to hurl insults. Of course, the umpire was the most irate of all. To him, the Travelin' Nine were delaying *his* game yet again.

He took his anger out on Dog.

"Get that mutt off *my* field!" he ordered the group of ushers gathered in the stands behind home plate. "Remove him from *my* stadium."

The ushers charged onto the pitch. However, they couldn't catch the crafty canine. Constantly changing directions, Dog outsmarted and outmaneuvered the attendants. And the hound seemed to be enjoying himself too, wagging his tail ever faster during the chase.

"Well done, Dog," Griffith said.

Griffith understood exactly what Dog was doing. The elusive hound was creating a diversion, distracting the ushers so that they wouldn't pay attention—at least for a few more minutes—to the three kids in the dugout.

"STRIKER TO THE LINE!": *what the umpire announced at the start of each contest. It was also called out at each batter's turn. Today, the umpire yells, "Batter up!"*

Finally, the winded and weary ushers caught up to Dog, but only because he had sat down on the mound.

"Go with these men," Preacher Wil instructed, wiping some of the snow from Dog's snoot. "Wait for us at the trolley stop. We'll meet you after the game."

Dog nodded at his owner and then headed off.

"Striker to the line!" the umpire barked

as soon as the ushers left the field with Dog. "Play ball now!"

Splat!

A large snowball hit Graham right on the cheek.

"Gotcha!" roared Griffith. He slapped his leg and hopped in a circle. "I can't begin to tell you how long I've been waiting to do that. Dad would have never let me hit you with—"

Splat!

An even larger snowball hit Griffith on the side of the head.

"Gotcha!" Ruby raised a triumphant fist.

"No way are you getting away with that!" Griffith declared while gathering a mound of snow. "No way!"

"Wait!" Graham suddenly shouted, jumping between his siblings. "Not no way, *snow* way!" He motioned to the field. "Preacher Wil should throw snowballs just like Happy threw fireballs in Chicago!"

"Good thinking, Graham!" Happy called from the end of the dugout.

"Great thinking!" Griffith agreed, shaping the pile of snow and plopping it on Graham's head. "Gotcha again!" He laughed.

Ruby immediately waved to Preacher Wil. When she caught his attention, she held up a single finger and pointed it downward—that was a catcher's signal for a fastball—and then sprinkled snow over her balled fist. Next she gathered her brothers and directed their hands to the baseball.

"Back to business, boys," Ruby ordered.

"Snow time!" cheered Graham.

On the hill, Preacher Wil scooped up a pile of snow (which was still coming down as hard as ever) and buried the rock within. He stared down the Millers' first striker, Kid McNeely, and slung the snowball. The hometown hitter swung meekly, popping the ball up to the infield.

"I got it!" Bubbles called, as a gloveman always should.

Pop.

One hand down.

Griffith gazed into the stands behind the dugout and then peered over at the rooters behind home plate. When those ushers returned, he thought, that's where they'd be. But so far, Dog was doing his duty.

GLOVEMAN: *fielder.*

HAND DOWN: *an out.* ONE HAND DOWN *meant "one out,"* TWO HANDS DOWN *meant "two outs," and* THREE HANDS DOWN *(or* DEAD*) meant "three outs."*

CHIN MUSIC: *pitched ball intentionally thrown high and inside, near the batter's chin and neck.*

As Germany Smith stepped to the line, Preacher Wil tipped his cap in Ruby's direction. Then he turned his attention to the Millers' batter. But this time around, Preacher Wil's icy stare didn't unnerve the striker. So the southpaw hurler employed a different tactic.

Chin music!

Preacher Wil fired his first snowball up and in. It sent Smith sprawling and his cap and lumber flying. Standing back up, Smith wore a uniform covered with snow (though to him it looked like dirt and mud). He also wore a face of burning rage that announced to everyone in Nicollet Park that he'd be swinging for the fences on the next pitch no matter what.

Covering his smile with his leather, Preacher Wil gripped the baseball in his glove. It was time for a curveball. However, as he rocked into his delivery, his front foot slipped, and the magnificent snow-covered pitch, which was supposed to break over the outside corner and then dissect the dish, was

suddenly heading for the heart of the plate.

"No!" Graham shouted, spotting Preacher Wil's misstep. "Freeze!"

HOOK: *curveball.*

Just as Germany Smith cocked his bat and prepared to swing at Preacher Wil's off-its-mark hook, everything stopped.

16

★

Time Stands Still

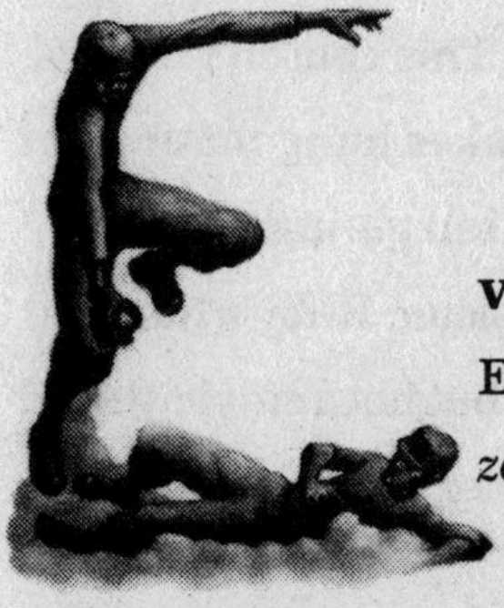

Everything stopped. Everything became *frozen* in time.

Preacher Wil's pitch halted in midair, halfway to home. Germany Smith's swing stopped behind his shoulders. On the Travelin' Nine bench, Happy had been clapping and shouting, but at the moment, he was motionless and silent. And down both foul lines and all through the stands, none of the cranks moved a muscle or uttered a sound. A total stillness had taken hold.

Except for one person. A single figure moved.

Graham.

"Whoa!" he said.

He grabbed his head with both hands and blinked his eyes as hard as he could. Then he blinked them again. This couldn't be real. Even the falling snowflakes hung motionless in the air. He had to be imagining it.

Graham spun to his sister. Ruby's hair was blown back by a breeze, but not a single strand was moving. He poked her in the shoulder.

No reaction.

He whirled toward Griffith. His older brother had his hand cupped around his wide-open mouth. When time had stopped, Griffith had been in the middle of a cheer. Graham reached out and poked him, too.

Nothing.

Graham smiled mischievously. "Time for a little payback," he said, scooping up a large mound of snow. "Sorry, Griff. I might never get an opportunity like this again." Then he reached up and dropped the snowball on top of his brother's head.

Griffith didn't bat an eyelash.

Stepping away from his siblings and out of the dugout, Graham trudged through the snow over to the cranks seated in the first row. He shook a man's hand, tried on a woman's feathery hat, and reached into a small boy's bag of peanuts.

Not a peep from anyone.

Graham headed for the Millers' bench, where the ballists stood as still as statues. He first approached Jay Andrews, leaning on his lumber in the on-deck area. He walked right up to the home team's third bag man and tugged on his beard. Then Graham shuffled over to Roger Bresnahan, stretching on the dugout steps, and crawled between the backstop's legs. When he stood up, Graham found himself face-to-face with Walter Wilmot. Graham glared long and hard at the Millers' manager. Then he reached over, lifted up Wilmot's cap, and placed it back on his head sideways.

None of the ballists budged.

Graham peered out at the field. "Hello!" he called. "Can anyone hear me?"

He stepped toward the pitch, but when he reached the area where he thought the first base line was, he stopped. Looking down, Graham wondered if setting foot into fair territory would for some reason start time again. He exhaled a long breath before slowly touching the toes of one foot between the white lines.

BETWEEN THE WHITE LINES: *on the playing field, in fair territory.*

Nothing changed.

Crossing onto the field of play, Graham headed straight for the pitched ball, suspended in midair between home plate and the pitcher's mound. He peeked over it, ducked under it, and then walked in a circle around it. He reached for the rock and was about to grab it, when he saw what had sprung up all along the outer garden wall. In an instant Graham was racing for right field, charging through the snow toward the frozen phenomenon.

"St. Anthony Falls," he said, gazing up at the Mississippi River's great waterfalls, which now somehow lined the outer garden.

Graham held his head again. How could this be? Was this really happening?

He inched closer to the once cascading waters, now frozen and unmoving. The ice was so clear, Graham was able to see all the way through. Without a doubt, there was something on the far side of the falls.

Lifting his hands from his head, Graham extended an arm and reached for the waters. He touched the frozen torrents with the tip of a single finger. The ice instantly melted at the point of contact.

"I have to be dreaming," he whispered.

Slowly, Graham inserted his fingers, then his hand, and then his arm into the waters. Everywhere he touched, the ice turned to flowing falls.

"I have to be dreaming," he repeated.

When the waters reached his elbow, Graham quickly drew back his arm. His jaw nearly struck his chest when he saw that his skin wasn't even damp. Not a single droplet of water remained anywhere.

Graham glanced over at Woody. The Travelin' Nine's immobile right scout stood in ready position, hands on knees, waiting for the striker to whip the willow.

"I am dreaming," Graham told himself, shaking his head. "I must be."

He turned toward the falls again. A surge of fear and excitement raced up and down his body. His touch melted the ice. Suddenly Graham realized that he could pass right through the waters. Leaning forward, he placed his face to the edge of the ice.

"Hello!" he called. "Anyone in there?"

He waited.

"Hello!" he called again.

Graham glanced over his shoulder at the field. Everyone and everything remained fixed in time. So Graham faced the water yet again, let out another long breath, and without hesitating, stepped all the way through St. Anthony Falls.

"Whoa!" he said, just as he had moments earlier.

Graham stood at the foot of a bridge, the same iron bridge he and the barnstormers had crossed on their way to Nicollet Park. He peeked over his shoulder. The frozen falls weren't visible from this side. Instead, a deep purple haze hovered over the grass, a haze that yellowed in the spot where he had passed through. Turning back to the bridge, he traced his fingertips along the familiar guardrail and peered out at the Mississippi River, the *still* Mississippi River, and the *real* St. Anthony Falls, also silenced and stopped.

Nothing was moving. While there was no snow or ice on this side of the St. Anthony Falls that Graham had passed through, everything here seemed to be suspended in time as well.

"Hello!" Graham yelled.

"Hellllllllooooooooo!" a distant echo replied.

Graham jumped. The sound of another voice startled him so that if not for the guardrail, which he managed to grab hold of, he very possibly would've toppled into the river.

Perhaps it was his own voice, Graham thought, once the shock of the moment subsided. Maybe it was just his echo.

"Hellllllllooooooooo!"

It was no echo. The returning voice was much deeper than Graham's. Without question, it belonged to someone else, and it was coming from downstream.

In a heartbeat Graham raced out onto the bridge. When he reached the middle of the span, he cupped his hands around his eyes and looked downriver at the mighty Mississippi. Not a ripple of current moved. Even the flock of gulls flying in formation were . . .

Then Graham spotted it. A single object floating on the still water. A lone man on a raft downriver was waving his hat in Graham's direction.

Graham tried to wave back, but the shock of the sight left him unable to lift his hands from his face.

"Dad," he said, although no sound left his lips. "Dad," he tried to say again.

The man continued to wave his hat, and then he shouted something, two unmistakable words.

"Dad!"

"Haaaaappy Birthdaaaaay!"

"Dad!" Graham shouted, the words erupting like a volcano. "Dad!"

Graham charged back across the bridge. When he hit the shoreline, he hurdled the guardrail and began racing along the bluff. But, reaching the edge, he stopped. The man and his raft had disappeared.

Suddenly Graham began to pant. Was all this real? He clutched his chest as he tried to catch his breath. Or was he dreaming? He didn't know. At this moment, the only thing he knew was that he *needed* to be with Griffith and Ruby.

Finding his wind, Graham tore back through the trees and burst from the woods. He charged toward the haze, and without slowing or breaking stride, he leaped through the yellowed section and back onto the fixed-in-time field. He raced through right garden, dashed over the diamond, and headed straight for his brother and sister.

But before crossing into foul territory, he skidded to a halt. Pivoting in the snow, he hurried back to the pitched baseball, still stopped in midair. With his eyes, he traced a path from pitcher to striker. Then Graham reached up and shifted the rock ever so slightly, so that it would no longer be right over the plate for Germany Smith to whack.

Graham clapped his hands once and then ran up to Griffith and Ruby. He slid in between his statuelike siblings, turned to the field, joined his hand with theirs on the baseball, and shouted:

"Snow time!"

17

★

Back in Play

rack! **Germany** Smith swung mightily, but he got under the ball. Instead of launching the rock over the fence, he lifted a towering, but routine, sky ball toward right-center garden.

"Comin' at ya!" Griffith shouted to Woody.

"Don't move!" added Ruby.

"Couldn't go anywheres if I wanted to!" Woody hollered back.

Knee-deep in a snowdrift, Woody could barely lift his boots. Fortunately, the blizzard

"Couldn't go anywheres if I wanted to!"

blew the baseball right to him. All he had to do was raise his glove.

Pop.

Two hands dead.

Griffith and Ruby cheered mightily, even as Griffith, with a puzzled expression, began wiping snow off his head. But Graham didn't shout along with his brother and sister. He was far too stunned. Except for the snow on Griffith's head, it was as if nothing had happened. Had it really happened?

"Are you okay?" Ruby asked, placing her hand on Graham's back.

Graham nodded.

"You sure?" Griffith said. "You look like you just saw a ghost."

Graham swallowed. Maybe he had. Or had he imagined everything?

"What's the matter?" Ruby pressed.

"Everything around me just stopped. Even you two." Graham looked from Griffith to Ruby. "And . . . and . . ."

And I walked out onto the field, and this frozen waterfall appeared, and I was able to pass right through it, and on the other side I saw Dad, and he . . . Even *he* couldn't believe this.

Graham sighed. Ruby was already beginning to eye him sideways, and Griffith was stroking his chin. As much as Graham wanted to tell his brother and sister about what had just happened, how could he? How could he possibly tell them about *whom* he had just seen? He knew what would happen. Ruby would tease him, and Griffith would worry about him even more than he already was. They'd both be even less likely to tell him what was really going on.

"Never mind." He sighed again. "I was just remembering this weird dream I had the other night. That's all."

"Are you sure you're okay?" Griffith asked.

"I'm sure," he replied. He pointed toward home plate. "We need to focus on the game."

Griffith turned to Ruby. "Actually, we need to go."

"Have they spotted us?" she asked.

Griffith shook his head. "Not yet, but I see them everywhere, and they're getting closer. We've pushed our luck far enough in here."

"Where will you go?" Happy inquired from his perch at the end of the bench.

"Leave that to me," Ruby replied, dropping the baseball into her pocket.

"You have a place in mind?" asked Griffith.

"Of course I do." Ruby flipped her hair. "Step quickly and stay low."

Looking both ways, as she would before crossing a busy street, Ruby led her brothers up the dugout steps and back into the stands. Ducking down so as not to block the view of the cranks, they wound through the bleachers.

"In here," Ruby called. She led her brothers into the narrow opening in the grandstands adjacent to the field-level boxes. "I saw this alcove earlier."

"It's just like the one we were in for the start of the game," Graham said. "In the outfield."

"Exactly," said Ruby. "I doubt they'll find us in here. And since we're so close to the players, we'll be able to help the barnstormers with the magic."

From their new vantage point, the three Paynes watched through gaps in the wooden slats as Preacher Wil recorded the last out of the frame, which also happened to be the easiest bug bruiser in baseball history. Because of the snow, the comebacker to the hill stopped at Preacher Wil's boots. All he had to do was reach down into the drift that had formed around his feet, pick up the pill, and throw it to the Professor.

Three hands dead.

"It ain't over till it's over," Ruby said, as

the barnstormers headed back to their dugout to bat the ninth.

"That's what you said back in Louisville," Graham said.

Ruby nodded. "That's what Uncle Owen liked to say, that's what I said back in the River City, and that's what all of us should say right now."

"It ain't over till it's over!" the three Paynes said as one.

All of a sudden, the Christmas miracle vanished. The snow disappeared.

And a new *sound* had begun to take its place.

	1	2	3	4	5	6	7	8	9	R
TN	0	0	0	0	0	0	0	0		0
MM	1	1	1	1	1	1	1	0		7

18

★

A Ferocious Comeback

he trio of ushers reached the dugout at the same time as the Travelin' Nine.

"Where are they?" barked the largest one. He searched under the bench and behind the barnstormers.

"Where are who?" Tales replied, hiding his smirk beneath his bushy mustache.

From the safety of the alcove, Griffith, Ruby, and Graham watched the drama in the dugout. But they were even more intrigued by the *gurgling* on the field.

With snow no longer blanketing the grass, the thousands of puddles that had dotted the field in the previous inning were visible again, and they all were gurgling.

"It's the land of ten thousand lakes," Griffith noted.

"But how are they going to help the barnstormers?" asked Graham. Then he cheered softly, "Come on, Bubbles!"

Ruby repositioned their hands on their baseball as the Travelin' Nine's shortstop stepped to the striker's line to lead off the final frame. When she did, the gurgling grew louder, and some of the puddles began to bubble. Those bubbling pools created a clear path from home dish straight into left garden.

"That's where Bubbles needs to hit!" Graham exclaimed.

"No doubt!" Griffith agreed, tousling his brother's hair.

Bubbles pounded the plate three times with his timber. Then he nodded in the direction of the umpire and backstop. But he was really acknowledging Griffith, who had briefly stuck out his head and nodded toward where Bubbles should hit.

Ruby aimed the baseball at left field and inserted her pinky into the acorn-size hole.

On the first pitch, Bubbles swatted a single past a diving Jay Andrews at third sack. The bounding ball skimmed from bubbling lake to bubbling lake, puddle-jumping into left garden.

"Here we come!" Graham declared.

With Bubbles standing at first bag and Guy making her way to the dish, the gurgling grew louder. And once again, some of the lakes started to bubble. But this time, they formed a route into right garden.

Guy pretended to politely greet her opponents, but like Bubbles, she was actually peeking at Griffith, who was leaning out and directing her to swing for right field.

On the delivery, Ruby inserted her pinky back into the baseball and pointed it toward right garden. Guy smacked Kid McNeely's first pitch, and the rawhide hopscotched from bubbling puddle to bubbling puddle. By the time Walter Wilmot chased it down, the Travelin' Nine had runners on the corners with nobody out.

RUNNERS ON THE CORNERS: *When base runners occupy both first base and third base, a team is said to have runners on the corners.*

"Two for two!" exclaimed Graham.

"And see who's batting next." Ruby motioned to Preacher Wil.

TWO DUCKS ON THE POND: *two men on base. The two ducks refer to the runners; the pond refers to the field.*

"Two ducks on the pond!" Griffith whispered. "Bring one home!"

"Look!" Ruby pointed.

Out in center garden, a large lake had taken over, just like the gigantic cow had back in Chicago. And in the center of that body of water, dozens of ducks swam in pairs, forming a circle and creating a target.

Dozens of ducks swam in pairs.

Preacher Wil didn't have to wait for any directions. Nor did he bother tipping his cap to the umpire. Like Bubbles and Guy before him, he swung at Kid McNeely's first pitch and drove the pill back up the middle. It splashed down in front of Jack Menefee amid the ducks on the center garden lake.

"Bull's-eye!" Ruby declared as feathers flew in every direction.

"You mean, *bird's*-eye!" Graham laughed over the quacking of the fleeing ducks.

"An RBI for Preacher Wil!" cheered Griffith.

The Travelin' Nine had seen only three pitches in the frame, but they already had three hits and their first run. And since Guy had motored all the way across to third, they had runners back on the corners.

Ruby smiled wide. Preacher Wil had managed his hit without the help of their baseball. She and her brothers hadn't aimed it, nor had she inserted her pinky in its hole. With the ballists united and determined, Ruby wondered if they even needed the extra aid of the magic baseball. But there was too much at stake. They couldn't afford not to try everything.

"I say we give Crazy Feet a hand," she said, lowering the baseball and repositioning her brothers' fingers.

"Look at this!" Graham cried. "We're moving the water!"

When the three hands on the baseball moved in one direction, so did the bodies of water on the field. If they moved the baseball to the left, all the lakes shifted toward left garden. When the three lowered their hands, all the pools moved toward the infield.

"Let's make a target for Crazy Feet," Ruby suggested, glancing at Griffith. "Where would you like to see him hit?"

Griffith sized up the field. At first base,

Perry Werden was playing off the line and behind the bag.

"Time for a little strategy," he said, lowering the baseball until the lakes were exactly where he wanted them on the infield.

"Great idea, Griff," Ruby agreed.

She stared at Crazy Feet and waited for him to tip his cap to the umpire and backstop. As soon as he turned to them, Ruby poked out her head.

BUNT: *soft and short hit, often to advance a runner.*

"Bunt," she mouthed to the Travelin' Nine's left scout.

Crazy Feet laid down a perfect one, pushing it up the first base line. By the time Perry Werden fielded the pill, Crazy Feet was racing past him and beating him to the sack.

"Yer out!" the umpire called. "One hand down!"

Griffith, Ruby, and Graham couldn't believe their eyes and ears. The Travelin' Nine should've had the bases loaded with nobody out, but the umpire had made yet another wrong call.

"That play wasn't even close," Griffith growled. "This umpire's not even trying to hide that he's favoring the Millers."

Although Crazy Feet had been retired, it was still a productive out. While Guy had to hold at third base on the play, Preacher Wil had moved over to second, placing two runners in scoring position.

SCORING POSITION: *Any time a runner is on second or third bag, he is considered to be in scoring position.*

But as Tales approached the plate, every last one of those ten thousand lakes on the field vanished. Not a single droplet of water remained on the green oasis.

"Where did they go?" asked Graham.

"Listen," Ruby said.

The three Paynes strained their necks and lifted their ears. The sound of rushing waters had returned.

Settling in at the dish, Tales flapped his elbow four times. Then, all of a sudden, the base paths between second, third, and home began filling with water. But these waters didn't flow like a river. They moved like an ocean tide.

"What do you make of this?" Ruby looked to Griffith.

He thought for a second and then snapped his fingers. "The runners need to ride the waves!"

"Go with the flow!" Graham cheered, wrapping his fingers around his sister's and making sure her pinky slid into the baseball.

Like Bubbles, Guy, Preacher Wil, and Crazy Feet, Tales swung at the first pitch. He smoked Kid McNeely's fastball toward the gap in right center garden. Bursting from the batter's box, Tales sped down the line toward first sack, and with each stride, ocean waters began to fill in underfoot.

"Catch a wave!" Ruby whispered.

Both Preacher Wil and Guy already had. Bodies flat, they crested the swells around the bases, riding the tides all the way home, to plate the Travelin' Nine's second and third tallies.

As soon as Tales saw what Preacher Wil and Guy were doing, he rode the waves too. He sailed to first bag and made a wide turn toward second. With his team down by so many, it was risky to try stretching a single into a double, but Tales had full faith in the flow. He glided safely into second sack.

"Seven to three!" Graham announced, pointing to the centerfield scoreboard. "It ain't over till it's over!"

Nicollet Park was buzzing. The crowd had just seen three ballists literally fly, bobbing in the air, around the bases.

Everyone responded to the tsunami-like shift in momentum. Frustrations mounted on the Millers' bench and escalated in the bleachers, too. No longer were the cranks shouting insults only at the Rough Riders; they were now hailing barbs at the hometown ballists as well.

"Go with the flow!"

Woody bolted to the line. With all the base paths filling with white-capped waves, he was eager for his chance to catch one. After pounding the plate and shuffling his feet into an ever-wider stance, Woody swung at offerings that were so far off the dish even this umpire may have called them balls. Because he didn't wait for directions from the three Paynes (or even give them a chance to aim their baseball), Woody struck out on pitches impossible to reach.

Two hands dead.

Still trailing by four runs, the Travelin' Nine were down to their final out. On top of that, all the waters left the field again.

"We have to focus as hard as we can," Griffith said to his sister and brother.

Ruby nodded once. She refused to allow any doubt to creep into her head. Not after all she had been through these last few days. And not with Scribe lumbering to the line.

With one whip of the willow, he could chop the deficit in half.

"He's going to hit one all the way to St. Anthony Falls," Ruby declared.

Scribe tipped his cap, pointed his timber to center garden, and dug in at the dish.

Wrapping her fingers around her brothers' on their baseball, Ruby inserted her pinky in the hole. Then she squeezed the baseball, lifted it up, and shot it forward.

"You know where to hit it," she whispered.

Like all the other barnstormers who had batted in the ninth frame, Scribe swung at the first pitch—a fastball right in his wheelhouse.

Boom!

The Travelin' Nine's mountain of a man blasted the ball high and deep to center garden. It soared way over the center scout's head, beyond the outer garden wall, and even over the scoreboard.

Home run!

WHEELHOUSE: *a hitter's power zone. Usually this is waist high and over the heart of the plate.*

"What a hit!" Graham whooped.

Griffith gazed out at where the ball had landed and shook his head. "I didn't know anyone could hit a ball that far."

"I knew he'd do it!" Ruby said.

At home plate, Tales and the other barnstormers greeted Scribe with handshakes and hugs. The titanic home run had trimmed the Millers' lead down to two.

"What do you say we give Doc a hand?" Griffith suggested to his siblings, as the eighth Travelin' Nine striker to bat in the inning beat his bowlegs at the plate.

Graham looked to his brother and sister. "What should we tell him to—"

Plunk!

Kid McNeely beaned Doc with a fastball.

All three Paynes gasped as Doc crumpled to the dirt. For a moment he lay motionless, and the barnstormers' hearts skipped a beat. But then Doc sprung like a spring, hopped to his feet, and sprinted down to first. As he took his base, he refused to rub the spot where the ball had hit his forehead.

"That was on purpose!" Graham exclaimed.

"That's dangerous!" yelled Ruby.

The umpire and backstop whirled around, but Griffith grabbed his sister and brother and pulled them back away from the wood before anyone spotted where the voices had come from.

FOUR-BAGGER: *home run.*

Griffith grumbled as he held on to Ruby and Graham. It was one thing to throw chin music like Preacher Wil had the inning before; skilled hurlers should be permitted to throw inside and move a striker off the plate. However, it was a whole other story when pitchers believed they should be allowed to use a hitter's head for target practice. Unfortunately, that was how some hurlers played nowadays. After a four-bagger, some pitchers felt the next batter's noggin was fair game.

"Look at it this way," Griffith said, as he let go of Ruby and Graham. "That may have been both intentional and dangerous, but now the Professor's bringing the tying tally to the plate."

"And Bubbles is on deck with the potential winning run!" Ruby added.

OPPOSITE FIELD: *the opposite side of the field from the one to which a batter naturally hits. A right-handed batter going the other way hits the ball to right field; a left-handed batter hits the ball to left field.*

Professor Lance stepped to the line and saluted Kid McNeely, but the Millers' hurler was in no mood for pleasantries. Then the Professor tipped his cap to the umpire and catcher, but they couldn't be bothered either. The Professor shrugged, tapped his lumber on the dish, and prepared for the pitch.

"Let's aim the ball again," Graham suggested.

"Sounds like a plan," said Ruby. She looked to Griffith. "Where to?"

Griffith thought for a moment. "Opposite field."

The three Paynes held their baseball as

tightly as they ever had. Then Ruby inserted her pinky into the hole, and the three pointed toward right garden.

"Strike one!" the umpire called on a pitch that bounced in front of the dish.

Graham growled. Ruby shook her head. Griffith pounded his leg.

"Strike two!" the umpire cried on a pitch that the backstop had to leap for.

Ruby peered over at the Travelin' Nine dugout. The ballists stood in a line on the top step. All eyes were glued to the green oasis. And Tales the talking mustache was giving the play-by-play.

Suddenly, and unexpectedly, Ruby smiled. "Everything is right," she said, looking back at her brothers. "The barnstormers don't need magic to help them win. They're united against a team of awful sports. Trust me, everything is more than right."

Crack!

The three pointed toward right garden.

"Line drive, base hit going into right garden!" Tales announced. "Doc Lindy races around second and heads for third, as Walter Wilmot gives chase in the corner."

"Go, Doc!" cried Ruby.

"Go, Lindy!" Graham cheered.

Griffith clutched his brother and sister. In their excitement, both had nearly burst onto the field.

"The Professor makes the turn around first and heads for second," Tales continued his call. "Wilmot's got the pill in right and fires it to the cutoff. Doc Lindy is rounding third. He's going to try to score the tying run. We're going to have a play at the plate! Here's the throw. Doc slides. Bresnahan fields the throw in his bare hand. He lunges for Doc Lindy with his mitt. . . . Safe! Tie game!"

"Yer out!" the umpire shouted, pointing to the catcher's mitt. "Game over! Millers win!"

"He never tagged me with the ball!" Doc cried, leaping to his feet. "He tagged me with his glove!" He pointed to the Millers' backstop, who still held the pill in his bare hand.

"My word is the final word," the umpire barked. "How dare you question my authority!"

"Can he do that?" asked Graham, placing his hands on his head. "That's cheating."

Ruby opened her mouth to answer, but she was too stunned by the abrupt ending to form words.

Griffith shook his head in disgust and disbelief. "The Travelin' Nine may have lost," he said, "but the Millers sure didn't win."

	1	2	3	4	5	6	7	8	9	F
TN	0	0	0	0	0	0	0	0	6	6
MM	1	1	1	1	1	1	1	0	X	7

19

★

The True Meaning of "Team"

Even though the Travelin' Nine had just suffered a difficult defeat, there wasn't a single glum face in their dugout.

"We took on a team of professional ballists today," Doc Linden addressed his teammates, "though one could argue they didn't act like professionals."

"Neither did the umpire," Bubbles inserted.

"But despite their behavior," added

Professor Lance, standing next to Doc, "we showed class and dignity. We afforded this great game the respect it deserves. And most importantly, we came together as a team."

"You sure did," Ruby whispered to herself.

The Travelin' Nine hadn't bothered asking the Millers to join them for the postgame gathering. Not that they'd had the opportunity. As soon as the umpire had declared the final out, the Millers had collected their gear and paraded from Nicollet Park. Everyone else followed—the cranks, the ushers, and the umpire.

Elizabeth stepped forward. "At times these last few days, we've disagreed," she said, removing her cap and shaking out her hair. "But we had the strength and courage to become one again."

"Indeed," said Happy. He hoisted himself from the bench and drew a circle in the air around all the barnstormers. "This here is the true meaning of 'team.'"

Griffith scanned the Rough Riders. They may not have been wearing their disappointment on their faces, but Griffith could still tell they all felt this was the toughest defeat to date. They had come so close to pulling off a miraculous, come-from-behind win. And if they had, because of the enormous turnout, they would've raised more money than at all their previous stops put together. They would've been well on their way to earning the ten thousand dollars needed to pay off Uncle Owen's debt.

However, the Chancellor had played dirty. He had switched the opponent to a team of professionals at the last minute. He had found an umpire who was willing to help fix the outcome. And he'd made the match winner take all, since he knew the barnstormers wouldn't stand a chance (even though they did almost prevail).

The Chancellor had orchestrated the entire day. Everything. The Chancellor wanted the Travelin' Nine to fail. He didn't want them to raise the money. But why?

Griffith grabbed the back of his neck as one final devastating thought popped into his head. The old man's haunting words:

There is one amongst you who cannot be trusted.

As much as he didn't want to believe it—as painful as it was—Griffith could no longer dismiss it. There was a mole on the team. One of the Travelin' Nine was working for the Chancellor. Griffith felt his frown deepen as he looked over at Ruby. His sister knew it also. The old man had confirmed what she had been thinking for some time now. Griffith pressed his palms to his temples. Who was it? Why would he betray everyone?

"I'd like to say something." Graham stood up. He wore an unusually long face.

"What is it, Grams?" Ruby asked.

Stepping around Scribe and over Dog, he climbed onto the top step. His glum face disappeared, and in its place was his mischievous smile, which he was unsuccessfully trying to fight off.

"I am very sad," Graham said, attempting to frown, but not doing a good job. "Today was the last time I'll get to see a baseball game as a seven-year-old. Saturday's game in St. Louis is on my birthday!"

"Happy birthday!" Woody cheered.

"Not yet," said Graham, holding out both hands. His fake frown was now a glowing grin. "Four more days."

Woody hopped up on the bench, but he had to hunch over so as not to hit his head. He draped one arm around Graham and gestured to his teammates with the other. "I reckon in

"I am very sad."

four days, after our victory in St. Louis, we're gonna have ourselves a birthday bash like no other for this here eight-year-old!"

"HUZZAH!": *common cheer to show appreciation for a team's effort.*

"Huzzah!"

20

★

Something About Grammy

om, I want to talk to you about Grammy," Griffith said, slipping into the seat across the table from her at the end of the dining car. "I'm worried about his birthday."

"Saturday may be a difficult day for him without your father," she pointed out. "He doesn't realize that."

Griffith leaned into the aisle and peered over his shoulder. The others were still eating, but Griffith had wolfed down his dinner as fast as he could. He knew his mother had asked to dine by herself so that she could write to Uncle Owen, but this couldn't wait. She needed to hear this.

"I don't think he understands what happened to Dad," Griffith explained. "He said something really strange to Ruby and me."

"What did he say?" Elizabeth placed her fork on her plate.

Griffith glanced down. Under the table, Dog brushed up against him and rested his head on his leg.

"He thinks Dad's coming back for his birthday," Griffith said.

The color drained from Elizabeth's face. "He said that?"

"I don't mean to upset you. I just—"

"No, Griff," she interrupted. She reached across the table and touched his face. "I'm glad you told me. Very glad. It's something I need to know."

Griffith nodded. "That's what I thought you'd say."

"And if he ever says anything like that again," she added, "tell me right away. Griff, sometimes even I lose sight of how difficult this must be for the three of you."

Griffith shut his eyes. At moments like these, he realized just how much he missed his father. So much that it hurt. So much that it nearly made him cry. That was why he tried not to think about his father. But he wanted to think about him.

Pulling back the shade, he leaned over and peered out the window. As the train left the city limits, the attendants had lowered all the shades on its western side because of the blinding rays that made it over the tops of the rolling plains this time of day. But no more. Most of the sunlight had faded. The landscape had turned to a burnt orange and was gradually disappearing into night.

Griffith glanced down.

The team had waited an extra day for this train to St. Louis. Instead of rushing to the station right after the game, the barnstormers had opted to stay until the next evening. This express train would have them at their next city in less than twelve hours.

"Keep an even closer eye on Graham," Elizabeth continued.

"I will. I'll tell Ruby as well."

She stroked his cheek. "I'm blessed to have such caring and resilient children."

Beneath the table, Dog lifted his head from Griffith's leg. His ears perked up, and he seemed to nod.

Elizabeth stole a glance over Griffith's shoulder as if she was checking to see that the others weren't close enough to hear what she would say next.

"Griff, I want you to know something else," she said after a long breath. "I've heard everything you've said to me these last couple of weeks about the Chancellor."

"You have?" Griffith was stunned to hear his mother say the name.

"Yes. I know you think he's behind all this. I want you to know that—"

Crash!

The door behind Elizabeth burst open. Three men in suits charged in. Two of them were yelling. One was waving a gun.

21

★

Grab Him, Grab It

rab him!” the intruder with the gun shouted, as the three men stormed down the aisle past Elizabeth, Griffith, and Dog.

“He’s the one!” a second man yelled, pointing toward Graham. The man’s hat flew off as he charged past the passengers and players.

When they reached the center of the car, the third man, the largest of the trio, dove across a table for Graham.

As dishes and glasses crashed and shattered, the handful of other passengers in the dining car gasped and screamed. But none of the Travelin' Nine moved. The sudden commotion had caught them off guard, and no one understood exactly what was happening.

"I got him!" the large man roared. Sprawled across the table, he held the youngest Payne by the arm and tugged him into the aisle.

"Nobody move!" the armed man barked. He pounded a table with his left fist as he waved the gun about in his right.

"Graham!" Elizabeth shrieked.

Ignoring the order, she sprung to her feet and raced his way. Griffith and Dog followed.

Dragging Graham down the aisle, the large man headed for the exit at the opposite end, while his two cohorts tailed close behind. Suddenly Scribe rose from his seat, took a giant step into the aisle, and stepped in front of the door. As large as he was, the man clutching Graham wasn't close to the size of Scribe, and as soon as he saw the hulking human blocking his escape route, the man lost his grip on Graham. The youngest Payne twisted free and dove under a table.

"Everybody down!" The man with the gun leaped onto a seat and waved it at the dining car.

The Travelin' Nine ducked for cover under the seats and on the floor. So did the other passengers. But not Elizabeth. Fearing they might grab Graham again, she tried pushing forward. Griffith and Dog followed. However, none of the three were able to maneuver past all the people on the floor.

Luckily, they didn't have to. Because of Scribe. With arms folded across his enormous chest, he stood firm in front of the door.

"Back that way!" the hatless bandit shouted.

The man with the weapon pointed it at the door where they had entered. "It's only two cars to the end. Run!"

Leaping over seats and plowing through passengers, the three bandits charged down the car. As he ran from table to table, the large man nearly clipped his head on a ceiling fan, though he didn't even notice. The hatless man kicked at Tales and shoved Bubbles to the floor, when both men reached for the fleeing felons. And the man with the gun lowered his shoulder and barreled past Elizabeth, Griffith, and Dog.

Then they spotted the *other* person they were seeking. She sat in the corner, cowering under a seat, desperately hoping not to be noticed.

"Grab it!" the largest man ordered.

The man with the gun whirled back around and pointed the weapon down the aisle at the ballists in pursuit. "Nobody move!"

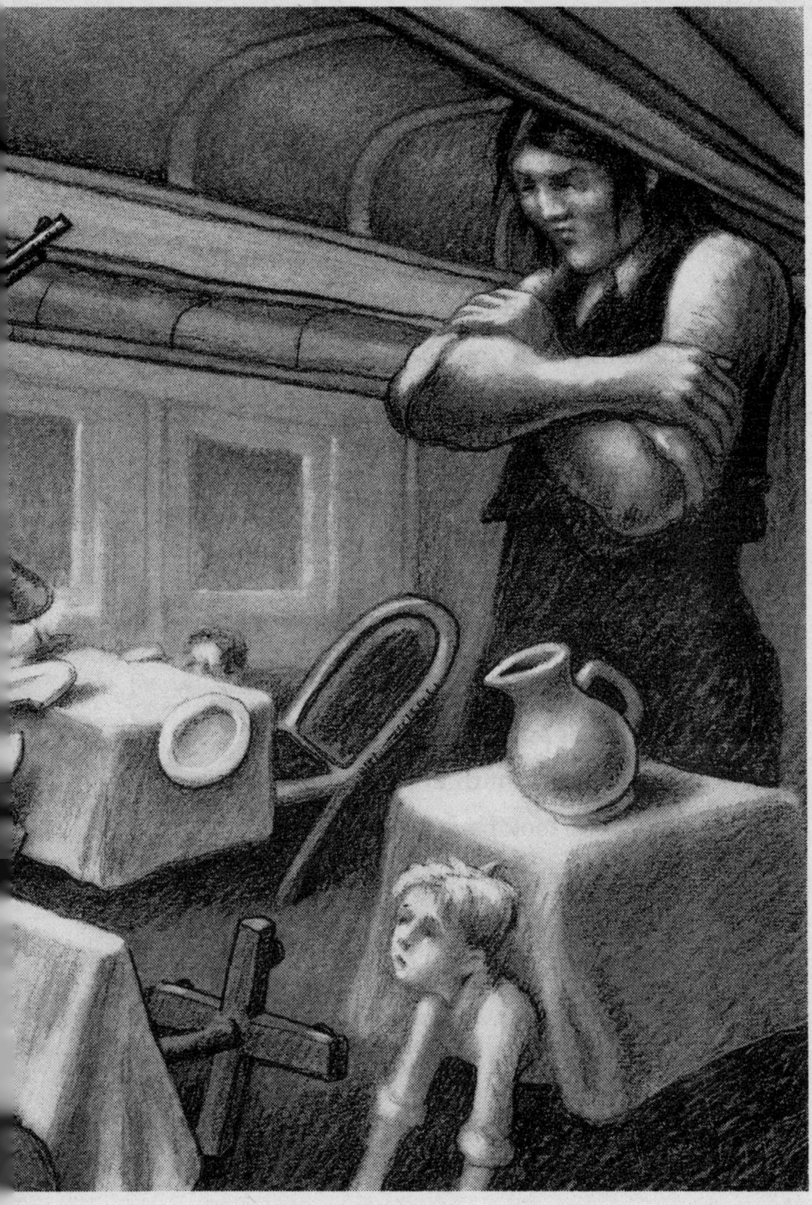

"Everybody down!"

"Ruby!" Elizabeth shouted, as she tried elbowing her way to her daughter.

Suddenly the hatless man dove to the floor and grabbed Ruby by the hair. He yanked her head back with one hand and started patting her down with the other. Then he ripped the baseball from her pocket.

"I got it!" he yelled. "Let's go!"

The bandits opened the door, fled the dining car, and raced toward the back of the train.

"Stop!" Griffith shouted, blowing by all the others and leading the pursuit.

But the men didn't break stride. Nor did they even look back.

"Last car!" the large man announced. He pulled open the door.

Griffith ran as fast as he could, reaching the door just as it was closing. He swung it wide, so that his mother, Woody, Preacher Wil, and all the others would catch it and not lose time in their pursuit. They would be right behind him when he reached the robbers.

Woof! Woof!

Out of nowhere, a *barking* Dog charged past Griffith. It was the first time Griffith had ever heard Dog bark, and it was a gigantic bark, a bark that meant business. He watched Dog close quickly, reaching the three henchmen just as they opened the final door and stepped onto the outside landing. Dog bit at the leg of the armed man, who tried to shake Dog free. When he couldn't, he raised the gun over his head.

"No!" Griffith yelled.

The man *hammered* the back of Dog's neck. Luckily, at the last possible moment, Dog recoiled, and instead of getting the full force of the metal, he was hit by the man's forearm.

Dog unlocked his jaws from the bandit, yelped in pain, and rolled over on his side.

"Dog!" Preacher Wil shouted.

Free of the canine, the armed man climbed over the chains and leaped from the speeding train. The large man followed, straddling the chains and tumbling off.

"They're getting away!" cried Griffith.

Only one bandit remained—the hatless one who still had the baseball. He stepped to the edge, climbed over the chains, and prepared to jump.

"Stop him!" Griffith shouted.

As if Griffith's words were a command, Dog scrambled to his paws and leaped at the robber at the very moment the bandit jumped from the train. In midflight, Dog latched onto the man's arm. The baseball popped free. As the two soared through the air, Dog's eyes never left the baseball, just as they'd never left the balls and sticks that Griffith had tossed when they played catch. Dog let go of the man's arm, snatched the baseball out of midair, tucked his chin to his chest, and tumbled to the ground.

"Dog!" Griffith and Preacher Wil screamed as one.

While the bandit fled, Dog sat down on the tracks. He held the ball in his mouth.

"Come on, boy!" Preacher Wil pleaded. He leaned against the chain railing and patted his legs.

Dog took one step forward. Then another. And another. But he was limping and couldn't run. So he lay down on the tracks and dropped the baseball between his paws.

Griffith grabbed his hair and pulled tightly. Then he did something that shocked even him. He straddled the railing and jumped off the accelerating train.

"Griffy!" Elizabeth screamed. "No!"

"Griffith!" called Preacher Wil. "Come back!"

. . . disappear in the distance.

But Griffith wasn't coming back. He tumbled to a stop, popped to his feet, and began running down the tracks *away* from the speeding train.

"Comin' through!" Woody declared. "I reckon we ain't leavin' that boy or that dog behind. A Rough Rider never forgets anyone."

Before a single other barnstormer could utter a response, Woody *also* leaped from the train. He rolled down a short incline, brushed himself off, and charged down the tracks.

"Woody!" Preacher Wil called.

"Griffy!" Elizabeth shouted.

"What happened to Griffy?" cried Ruby and Graham.

They reached their mother just in time to see Woody, Dog, and their older brother disappear in the distance.

★

See what's on deck!

Read a chapter from the Travelin' Nine's

next game in

BLASTIN' THE BLUES,

AVAILABLE FEBRUARY 2010!

★

Walking the Dark Tracks

"Don't say a word," Woody whispered, his finger pressed to his lips.

Griffith nodded once. He could feel his heart beating in his chest. With a trembling hand, he gently stroked the back of Dog's head. The Chancellor's thugs stood just yards away, and the faithful hound refused to stop his purrlike growling.

Under the cover of darkness, Griffith, Woody, and Dog huddled together in the thick brush by the side of the tracks. After leaping from the speeding train bound for St. Louis,

Woody had used the skills he'd honed fighting in the jungles of Cuba to steer them to this patch of high grass. So long as they remained silent and motionless, they would be safe.

Griffith looked up. Even in the pitch dark, he could make out the shapes of the Chancellor's thugs. He was able to hear their every word, too.

"We need to get out of these woods," one said.

"We need to find that baseball," said a second. "Boss man's gonna—"

"We're never going to find it out here!" the third thug cut him off. "I ain't staying in no woods all night."

"Boss man's going to have our necks when he learns we don't got it."

"That dumb dog got it." The first thug kicked at the ground.

Griffith covered his eyes from the spray of pebbles and dirt, while Woody leaned over and shielded Dog.

"I reckon city thugs ain't the same animal as wilderness thugs," Woody mouthed. He rubbed Dog's hind leg, the one he had hurt jumping off the train. "We're gonna be fine, Griff. Let's just wait 'em out."

Griffith nodded. He rubbed the scrape on his elbow, the only injury he had suffered from the leap.

"I ain't looking for no mutt out here," the first thug went on. "We'd run into a wolf or a bear wandering these woods."

"Boss man's going to be furious we didn't get the kid."

"To heck with the kid and that ball!" The first thug kicked the dirt again. "Too late to do anything about either one. Might as well go back now before some creature comes along."

The Chancellor's men headed off. In a matter of moments, their voices and footsteps could no longer be heard. Still, Griffith, Woody, and Dog remained in their hiding spot.

"If you ask me," Woody said softly as the minutes passed, "they're long gone." He rubbed the bruise on his cheek. "But I reckon we're gonna hold our position a little while longer."

Despite Woody's assurances, Griffith didn't believe they were entirely safe. The Chancellor's men could still be lurking in the woods, preparing to pounce. He tried to tell himself that Dog would've been growling if they were, but it didn't help. And the constant rhythms of the tree frogs and crickets, and the periodic hoot of an owl, also kept him on edge.

He ran his hand through his hair. The Chancellor's men had tried to *kidnap* Graham. Griffith had known the Chancellor was capable of anything, but in his worst nightmares, he'd never thought the Chancellor would order his thugs to try to *take* his little brother. The goons had tried to steal the baseball, too. They'd ripped it away from his sister. The Chancellor had instructed grown men to rough up a young girl.

Griffith slipped his still-trembling hand into his pocket and gripped the baseball. The attack had taken place more than an hour before, but he wondered if he would ever stop shaking.

"I still can't believe you jumped off that train," Woody said, as they headed down the tracks.

"I can't believe you jumped off either," Griffith replied, flinching as a rabbit or raccoon darted across the rails.

Woody smiled. "I wasn't about to leave you behind. A soldier never leaves another behind."

"It wasn't like I was alone. I had Dog with me."

Griffith reached down to pat the hound's

head, but the shriek of a bird caused him to recoil again.

Dog drifted over and brushed his snout against Griffith's pants. As they walked along, the canine favored his left hind paw. At times he raised it off the ground and used only three legs. Griffith wondered if Dog would be able to make it all the way back to Minneapolis.

When they'd started walking a short time ago, Woody had told Griffith and Dog that they would head back to the city. At the time they'd leaped from the train, they couldn't have traveled more than ten or twenty miles. While it would be a long trek, one that would more than likely take all night, it was the safest course of action, since they had no way of knowing if the next town was five or fifty miles ahead.

"You still worried 'bout them bandits?" Woody asked.

Griffith didn't answer.

"Well, I ain't gonna tell Griff Payne not to worry, because I know that won't do any good." Woody chuckled. "I reckon we focus on something else. Like that baseball. I'd like to see it."

Griffith reached into his pocket for the ball and handed it to Woody. Cradling it with both hands, the Travelin' Nine's right scout held the sphere to his face and examined it as closely as he could in the darkness.

SCOUT: *outfielder.: The right fielder was called the "right scout," the center fielder was called the "center scout," and the left fielder was called the "left scout."*

"I've only held this treasure in these here hands one other time," Woody said. "And believe it or not, I was walkin' the tracks just like this."

"Where was that?"

"Before heading off to Cuba, most of us were stationed in Tampa, Florida." Woody spoke softly and deliberately. "Thousands and thousands and thousands of soldiers all in one place. We Rough Riders came in from

San Antonio, but by the time we arrived, them train tracks was so clogged with freight cars, we had to get out and finish the journey on foot. Walked the tracks like we are now." Woody tightened his grip on the baseball. "It was durin' that walk that your pop let me hold this here baseball. The only time he did. And you know what he said to me?"

Griffith shook his head.

"Your pop made me a promise, Griff. Promised me my life. Promised all the Rough Riders our lives. Said we'd all return from Cuba." Woody lifted a hand from the baseball and raised a finger. "But he said there was one condition. You know what that was?"

"I do," Griffith replied, smiling.

On many occasions, his father had told him what he'd said to his fellow soldiers before heading off to war. They were the same words he so often said to Griffith and his sister and brother.

"Be together," Griffith said, gazing up at Woody. "Always."

Woody ran his fingers over his smile, then placed the baseball back into Griffith's hand.

"Uncle Owen gave us the baseball the night of the funeral," said Griffith, slipping the object back in his pocket. "He told us not to tell anyone we had it."

"I figured that's when y'all got it," Woody said, nodding. "But some of the others didn't think it showed up till Louisville or Chicago and—"

BARNSTORMERS: *team that tours an area playing exhibition games for moneymaking entertainment.*

"Wait," Griffith interrupted. "All the barnstormers knew we had the baseball?"

"'Course we knew!" Woody laughed. "We've known for some time. But we was all too amazed at how well you kids could keep a secret to say anything. A seven-year-old boy, a nine-year-old girl, and an eleven-year-old boy all kept their mouths shut." Woody laughed again. "Now, that's magic!"

Griffith thought back to the exchange he'd had with Happy in the dugout during the game in Minneapolis. Happy knew about their baseball; he'd made that perfectly clear. But what Griffith hadn't realized was that *all* the Rough Riders knew about it too. There was no need for secrecy when it came to the baseball (especially after what had just taken place on the train), and for the first time since the attack, Griffith felt a hint of relief.

He looked ahead and squinted his eyes. They had to have been walking for at least a couple of hours now, but the faint glow of lights from the city still didn't appear to be getting any closer.

"I reckon there's a bigger secret we need to deal with on this team," said Woody. "Scribe and I have been talking about it, and we're concerned that—"

"There's a mole on the Travelin' Nine," Griffith interrupted again.

Woody stopped. A wooden railroad tie cracked underfoot. "How do you know?"

Griffith could see the anguish on the Rough Rider's face.

"It's the only thing that makes sense," Griffith answered. "Ruby thinks so too." He swallowed. "And that's what the old man told us."

"The one you spoke about in the dugout?"

Griffith nodded. "We didn't want to believe it, but once the old man said what we were thinking, we couldn't deny it. It hurts so much to . . ." His words trailed off.

"It sure does," Woody said. "I reckon it's a hurt like I've never experienced. Never." He started walking again. "On the one hand, I'm so angry I want to grab this man by the throat. But at the same time, we're talking about one of us, a brother who served by our side in the war. It's heartbreaking." Woody pinched the bridge of his nose. "How can a member of your *family* betray you like this?"

Griffith frowned. It was as if Woody was speaking Griffith's own thoughts. And Ruby's, too.

There is one amongst you who cannot be trusted.

The old man's words echoed in Griffith's head.

"How are we going to figure out who the mole is?" asked Griffith.

Woody sighed. "It could be almost anyone."

"How do I know it's not you?"

Woody stopped again.

Griffith gasped. He couldn't believe that question had just left his lips. How could he be so disrespectful? But as he started to wish the words back, he caught himself, because a part of him was glad he'd been courageous enough to ask.

"I reckon you don't know it ain't me," Woody said. He turned to Griffith and rested both hands on the boy's shoulders. "But I offer you my word, Griff. Your pop made a promise to me, and I make a vow to you." He paused. "I am a man of honor."

Woody wasn't the mole. Griffith was certain. But it was more than merely his words that told Griffith that.

Some things you just know.

Griffith turned and looked up at the tracks. The moonlight reflected off the rails, two white lines pointing the way back to Minneapolis.

"We're gonna be spendin' a whole lot of time together these next few days, you and I," Woody said, draping an arm over Griffith's shoulder as they started walking again. "I reckon you're gonna get to hear all my war stories." He let out a short laugh. "Heck, by the time we make it to St. Louis, you're gonna know just 'bout everythin' that went on down there in Cuba."

"I'd like that," Griffith said. He reached

down to Dog and stroked his neck. "I'd like that a lot."

In the past, Griffith's father had tried to tell him stories from the battlefield, but Griffith had always made him stop. The only tales he was able to tolerate were the ones from San Antonio, when the Rough Riders had first met. Griffith didn't want to know about those days without food and water and those nights without sleep. Nor did he want to hear about all the brushes with death.

But that was before this summer. Now Griffith needed to know absolutely everything. What happened in Cuba could very well contain some of the—

Suddenly Dog's ears perked up. The hound glanced around and then gazed into the night sky, his eyes appearing to follow something in flight.

"What is it, Dog?" asked Griffith.

For a brief instant, he thought he saw

the outline of a moving object, but it quickly disappeared.

As dawn began to break, Griffith, Woody, and Dog finally reached the city limits. Because of the eerie fog hovering over the metropolis, the lights of Minneapolis had never seemed to get any closer as they walked back. But now daylight had brought the city into full view, and Griffith began to recognize some of the buildings, streets, and signs. He even spotted the bridge they had walked across on their way to the match in Nicollet Park.

MATCH: *baseball game or contest.*

However, when they neared downtown, Woody steered them from the tracks.

"Where are we going?" Griffith asked. "We need to go to the station to catch a train."

Woody shook his head. "I reckon you can't board a train without a ticket," he replied. "And how you comin' up with a ticket if you don't have any money?"

Griffith gulped. "I forgot about that."

“I didn’t.” Woody pointed ahead. “Let’s see if we can find ourselves a friendly face or two.”

Woody was leading them back to the university. Perhaps someone they’d met at the dorms or the library was still there. Maybe they’d be willing to provide them with food, a place to wash, and money for train tickets.

As they turned up the road leading onto campus and headed for the quadrangle, Dog held his head high. He recognized the spot where he and Griffith had played catch a few days earlier. Soon he was prancing, almost as if he was trying to tell the boy that his hind leg was completely healed. But Dog wasn’t ready to play. He was still limping, more than ever. Like Woody and Griffith, Dog needed rest.

Griffith peered in the direction of the dorms. Through the early morning fog, he spotted a figure standing by the front entranceway. He appeared to be staring back at Griffith, almost as if he was expecting a visitor. Griffith approached the silhouette, and the fog thinned, revealing the familiar and unforgettable face.